Musings
of a
Mystery Sibling

Bob,

I feel very bonded to you because of this deep loss we both live with, and I have to say that I think Peggy + Mike would be very proud of us.

Peace + love to you,

Mare

Musings
of a
Mystery Sibling

A Novel

Marian Armstrong

iUniverse, Inc.
New York   Bloomington

Musings of a Mystery Sibling
A Novel

iUniverse books may be ordered through booksellers or by contacting:
iUniverse
1663 Liberty Drive
Bloomington, IN 47403
www.iuniverse.com
1-800-Authors (1-800-288-4677)

Because of the dynamic nature of the Internet, any Web addresses or links contained
in this book may have changed since publication and may no longer be valid. This is a
work of fiction. All of the characters, names, incidents, organizations, and dialogue in
this novel are either the products of the author's imagination or are used fictitiously.

ISBN: 978-1-4502-3418-4 (pbk)
ISBN: 978-1-4502-3419-1 (ebk)
ISBN: 978-1-4502-3420-7 (hbk)

Printed in the United States of America
iUniverse rev. date: 7/21/10

For my siblings, all three of them.

~M.A.

"It is remarkable how closely the history of the Apple-tree is connected with that of man."

~Henry David Thoreau, "Wild Apples"

Chapter 1

An Introduction

Dear Ellen (if I may):

I am a bit of a slow bloomer, of which I am somewhat proud. In a world that relies more heavily on modern technology with each passing year, I have been happy to devote my days to an age-old art. I have spent my 78 years on an apple farm, my father's, and his father's before that. Although it is hard work, it needn't be done quickly. In part, it is a waiting game. Observing nature is key, and ripeness is celebrated. Up until recently, I have been enjoying what many refer to as "ripe old age." Like the goodness of a well-farmed apple, it is worthy of celebration. This I still believe.

I married late in life, and my first child, a boy, arrived the day after my fortieth birthday. This letter is very much about him and the ever-increasing gap between us. He is now my only child. My daughter, Judith, died in a motorcycle accident four years ago. Prior to that, I would have thought it impossible for the words Judith *and* motorcycle *to appear in the same sentence. She was a free spirit, but not one you would easily refer to as adventurous. She loved living, and*

1

trying new things came easily, but the word adventurous *lends itself to more risk-taking than Judith could easily muster. An investment banker, Judith was always about finding balance. She would try new things, within reason. She was my little girl. She came into this world a part of my flesh and bones, and it is incomprehensible to think that the mixture of those two things, the delicate balance that forms a body, has ceased to exist.*

Although I do my share of grieving in the quiet hours of the day, for now I will not dwell on Judith, as hers is a situation that cannot be helped. I write to fill the void that now exists in my family, to help my son come to terms with a death that is not his fault. His mother, long gone now, would want me to pull together these pieces, if it is the last thing I do. In some small way, she has led me to you. I have always been content to record my thoughts and observations on life in a journal, to be reviewed at some later date for my own amusement ... something funny that my wife said, my daughter's first steps, my son's graduation. I was always more of a listener, but now, in the autumn of my life, it is a race against time to be heard. I'm not really sure why, but it brings me comfort to know that it is at least possible that someone is reading my words. You do not know me, and this too brings me comfort. I require no response from you, nothing at all. You are a forum for me to freely express my thoughts, and I will trust that you don't mind. Should this be something that frightens you, throw my letters away and I will never know.

Clem

His letter transported me. For a while I could do nothing but sit back and appreciate the stillness of the room. It was the end of what had been a long, hectic, and mostly meaningless day in early June, almost four years to the day after my brother's death, and the warm sun was finally beginning to nestle into Manhattan's West Side skyline. It was unclear to me if it was the unusual pink glow cast on the room or something about his letter that made all my personal and professional mementos, the items that signified a moderately successful fifteen years as a book editor, seem foreign to me. I was more or less astonished that his words had struck a chord of sincerity that pierced me, that they were able to convey a frightening depth of sorrow, one that mirrored my own.

Chapter 2

Ellen's Story

For some, the light at the end of the tunnel is a sign of hope. For me, it is a symbol of eternal darkness. Every morning and evening I subject myself to its presence on the platform of the # 6 train. If I am late, I race toward it, my legs as fast as the cranks on a high-powered locomotive. If I am early, I reverently watch the glow of the light get brighter, knowing that I will ultimately allow the force of the train's arrival to suck me in and spit me out within a fraction of a second. It is a sick form of honor, one I don't share with anyone. It has been four years now since my brother was pushed from the platform, and perhaps I should be a regular passenger again, to let this ritual die too, but there is nothing regular about my life anymore. The victim of a deranged individual's thrust, he was the last living member of my immediate family. Observers of my life said that anger would eventually set in, and for a long time I feared it. It never came.

Will it ever? I don't know. But I'm not afraid of it anymore. Its arrival is not as impending as the relentless light at the end of the tunnel.

☐

I remember everything about the call that came late morning on a Thursday. It's funny how you always remember the smallest details of your life before it changes forever.

"Ellen Bannister?" a soft male voice inquired.

"Speaking," I replied.

"This is T. J. Clarke. I'm a detective with the NYPD, the 19th precinct. I need to discuss a highly confidential matter with you in person, if that's all right. Would it be okay if I stopped by your office in a little while?"

The voice, although somewhat apologetic, was steady and sure, and I immediately got the sense that any attempt on my part to obtain more information over the phone would be futile. I pressed anyway, figuring he's asking a lot and offering little in return. "A confidential matter related to what?"

His reply was quick and firm, leaving little room for further interjection. "I really can't discuss it over the phone, Ms. Bannister. I'm sorry. I'll be there shortly."

As I heard him hang up, it occurred to me that he never asked where he was going or how he could find me. I instantly went in search of Julie, the only one in our office capable of making the gravest of situations seem light as air.

"A detective is coming to talk to me," I whispered as I leaned over her desk. I paused for her reaction, but she waited to hear more. "What do you think he could want with me?"

Realizing that I had no story, she made one up. "Maybe Mrs. Bertelsman croaked and left you oodles of dough." I had mentioned to her that morning that I was mildly concerned that I had not seen my ninety-four-year-old neighbor in several days. Julie's eyebrow arched as she said it, and one side of her mouth puckered as if she had just solved the crime mystery of the century, and now, having done so, she could return to what she was doing.

"Seriously, Jules, what could he want with me?"

"I don't know. How do you even know he's really a detective? Probably some guy who thinks you're a hottie, and he wants to be your butterscotch stallion," she said with a wink and a giddy-up tongue clucking. "Ride 'em, cowgirl! HEE-HAW." And this was meant to comfort me.

She had a way of retreating from the issue at hand, of going in a million different directions. It was a quality I both admired and disdained, but at the moment a temporary retreat from reality was welcome. She had infused the unknown with excitement, and I began to feel my spirits lift. For some reason, I was important enough to be paid a visit, and I began to find some satisfaction in it. I swaggered back to my office, finding solace in my personal invention that perhaps I was unwittingly the crucial and elusive link to an unsolved crime that Detective Clarke had been working on for years. My dream, and my comfort zone, didn't last long. Julie's voice blared out from the phone intercom, "He's heeeere."

As I approached to shake his hand, he took me in quickly with his eyes. I was sure I detected a glance at my ring finger. Although it was easy to see that this wasn't his finest moment, he had the demeanor and appearance of a man who was comfortable with himself.

"Ms. Bannister, is there somewhere we can speak privately?"

"My office should offer all the privacy we'll need," I answered, gesturing the direction with the wave of my arm as I began to walk.

"Thank you."

Safely tucked within four walls and a closed door, Detective Clarke softened somewhat. "Are you married, Ms. Bannister?" he asked sympathetically. It wasn't exactly a loaded question, but the answer didn't come easily to mind. Now I was the one looking at my ring finger. The skin once sheltered by a band was soft and pale. Technically the answer was still yes, but my heart and soul begged to differ with it.

"What is this about, Detective?" I asked wearily.

"I'm afraid I have to reveal that sooner than I care to. Please," he entreated, "are you married?"

"Yes," I replied, reluctantly.

"To John Bannister of 1600 Third Avenue?"

"No," I said softly, beginning to feel the bottom drop out of my stomach. He looked at me inquisitively. "He's my brother," I said.

"Ma'am, I'm very sorry to have to tell you this …" He continued with what he had to say, but I did not want to process anything past "Ma'am." I clung to it nervously, wondering why I had suddenly been elevated to such a status by a man who had to be fifteen years my senior. The words *pushed, platform, deranged individual, internal trauma* began to perform a dizzying dance in my head. I pushed myself to concentrate, and then to convince the detective that he had to be wrong.

"No, I just spoke to him," I begged.

"When?"

"Last night. He was doing his laundry."

"This happened this morning, Ms. Bannister, at approximately 7:45," he gently insisted as he slid a business card across my desk. I picked it up gingerly, horrified that it was mine. It was well worn. I didn't remember giving it to John. I can only guess that I wanted him to fax me something, since that part of the card had been circled.

I don't remember how long I looked at it, but I remember my eyes eventually searching for Detective Clarke's. "What now?"

"When you're ready, I'd like to take you to the medical examiner's office for official identification of the body. You won't have to see him," he immediately offered, for which I was grateful, although it baffled me. He went on to say that identification in such cases was often through photographs, and that he hoped it brought me some relief to know that his face was unmarred. Such a bizarre thing to hope; was all I could think, but I knew he meant well. "Is there anyone you would like to accompany you … a family member, a friend?"

I began to attempt sorting names in my head, feeling a fresh sickness when I realized that John's name was first on a very short list. *Yes, I had to notify John about his own death. Let me write that down on my to-do list.* The absurdity of the situation, the improbability of it all, began to creep back to the forefront of my mind. Eight million people live in New York City, and Detective Clarke means to tell me that John was the one among all of them standing in the wrong place at the wrong time? Yes, he took the train every day. This much was true. On lucky occasions our paths would cross, me with my coffee, John with his newspaper. He would tease me about how unnecessary my morning pick-me-up was now that I was in his presence. I could never admit that it was partially true. The need to contact him resurfaced several times as Detective Clarke waited patiently.

"He has a fiancée," I finally said. "I should probably call her." I picked up the receiver and dialed John's work number, hoping against all hope that he would answer and that I could apologize to Detective Clarke for making his life harder but that he had the wrong John Bannister. One ring, then two. After the third, his voice mail picked up. His message, warm and personable, was the epitome of who he was. He was sorry that he was not available at the moment to take the call, but he would be happy to return it if the caller was inclined to leave their name and number. He hoped the caller was having a nice day. *Oh God, John, if you only knew!*

My business card, all 3 x 2 inches of it, loomed large in my hand. It was the part I couldn't explain away. And then I realized there was more. "How did you know his address?" I asked, beginning to think that perhaps I should go with Detective Clarke. I could always try to reach Katherine from the medical examiner's office, that is, if there was a need to do so.

"It was on his driver's license, Ma'am."

His words cut right through me, as deep and hotly intense as any metal wheel slicing through flesh. As painful as the realization was, I could not bring myself to cry. I was tired, exhausted even. I needed fresh air. "Why don't we go now?" I said, somehow finding my legs under the chair.

"Of course," he said as he rose swiftly, exhaling as he did so, I suppose relieved. He followed me down the hall and out into the reception area. I stupidly pressed the UP button, not realizing I had done so until his arm reached quietly behind me to press DOWN, and we waited what seemed an eternity.

At some point my eyes met Julie's. Lines I had never seen on her were burrowed into the inside corners of her eyebrows as she mouthed, "Are you okay?"

"Fine," I replied, stepping into the elevator, trying to sound convincing. "I have to step out," I yelled back, holding the elevator door briefly. "I'll call you later, Jules." I was eager to get outside. It was as if I thought the sunlight would change everything.

For whatever reason, there are large chunks of time that have slipped from my memory, or perhaps were never a part of it to begin with. The things I remember from here on are strange and isolated from each other, pieces of a puzzle, so many others missing. I remember seeing the new book designer with the black retro eyeglasses leaning against the building, taking a long drag on his cigarette in the midday sun. And I remember Detective Clarke, signaling to a fellow detective to drive the car up to us, streams of sunlight straight as arrows bursting from behind the sleeve of his blazer.

The medicinal green paint of the medical examiner's office and the Formica desktops encased in chrome bands also hold their place in my memory, their effect oddly soothing. There was no need for fashionable updates. Clearly no one was interested in aesthetics. With all a visitor might have to deal with at a medical examiner's office, contending with an air of pretension need not be a concern. There was no sitting around as a patient might at a doctor's office, wondering, ultimately, will he or she be the one paying for the Tiffany vase lodging fresh-cut flowers. At the medical examiner's office I could easily slip into the past, which is where I wanted to be anyway.

There was a lot of paperwork to sort through, lots of questions that needed to be asked, and frequently, "Are you all right, Ms. Bannister? Can I offer you a cup of coffee, a glass of water?" For proceedings of a clerical nature, I had been temporarily transferred to the consummate care of another officer, yet Detective Clarke flew in and out of the room with the regularity of a hawk feeding a nestling. He eventually escorted me back to the main entrance, where peripherally I could see a tall figure rising from a seat across the room.

Detective Clarke led me with all the care of a military officer at a presidential funeral, only there were no dignitaries here, no cameras to document his actions. Because he was not a warm man, it was easy to overlook his decency. He wanted me to meet Officer George Nichols, the first officer at the scene, and the two of them spoke to me at length about what had happened.

Questions plagued me, all of which they anticipated and attempted to address as they sat me down in a quiet corner of the lobby, the officer gently taking my hand. "It all happened very fast," he insisted. "Your brother died instantly. He was pushed directly into the path of an oncoming train. There was no time to think about what was taking place. You know what he was probably thinking about?" he said retrospectively as he slid a folded newspaper out of a clear plastic baggy. "My guess is that he was thinking about last night's game between the Mets and the Yankees, because this is what he was holding in his hand."

I began to feel the tears pool underneath my eyelids at the very sight of the sports section. "A Subway Series," I blubbered out, sobbing and laughing at the same time. I looked up to see that they were both stunned into speechlessness.

There was an awkwardness for a second or two, and I waited to hear more. Officer Nichols finally hung his head and chuckled, squeezing my hand as he did so. He then raised his head, looked me squarely in the eyes, and said, "I walked myself right into that one." There was a peculiar desire to laugh, but the laughter made me feel sick, like I was betraying one of the great loves of my life. How could I ever explain to John that I had laughed at the medical examiner's office? The officer was not to blame. I had set the tone for it.

"It's okay, Ms. Bannister," he assured me, reading my mind. "A mixed range of emotions is normal. The laughter is just a healthy release."

"Maybe I should see him now," I said. I didn't want to, but it was hard to forget that it was the main reason I was there. I wanted to be near him and as far away as possible at the same time, the way I felt a lifetime ago before being dropped off for my first-ever sleepover. I wanted to throw my arms around my mother and tell her how much I would miss her, Pop, and "Johnnie," as we called him back then. I wanted her advice on how to keep the butterflies from flying out of my mouth without my ever having to acknowledge that they were really there. If only I could have slipped under the throw rug and seeped into an unnoticed crack in the oak floor of my friend's foyer until Mom and Johnnie left. That way I wouldn't have to perform quick reassuring glances back and forth, one intended to prove to Mom that I was totally okay with her leaving me while the other was to speak volumes to my friend about how excited I was to be with her. Ultimately the conversation regarding the arrangements for pick-up went on too long, and there was a giggle and then an impatient tug on my arm. A goodbye muttered too quickly was the pervasive theme of my life.

John and I did not attend our parents' funeral. Aunt Celia stayed home with us, thinking it best not to put "the children" through it. "Hadn't they been through enough already?" she asked friends and neighbors alike as she retold the story again and again over the years. I knew her heart was in the right place, but I always felt that we should have been there. Goodbyes were never given the justice they deserved in our family, and we as children were expected to slide comfortably from our own home to our aunt and uncle's without ever verbally conceding what a transition it was for us.

"I'll go get the photo from the medical examiner," said Detective Clarke.

"No, wait. I'd really like to spend a minute with the body please."

"Ma'am, you don't want to do that," said the police officer, sympathy embedded in every crease of his black forehead. The words hung somewhere between a question and a declaration, but the silence that followed indicated that he waited for a response.

"Ms. Bannister, I will have full reports written up," said Detective Clarke. "You can refer to them anytime you like." He paused for a second and then said, "I'll go get the photograph."

I knew they were trying to tell me not to act too hastily, that what I could see may haunt me forever. I didn't want to remember John in bits and pieces. I didn't want his dignity stripped, yet I wanted to offer him the reverence he so justly deserved. I was no longer the child who didn't have control over my actions. I would have no one to blame later for steps not taken.

I weighed the situation carefully as Detective Clarke returned with the medical examiner, a white-cloaked woman of about fifty. She shook my hand and told me how sorry she was, and then she slid a single photograph from an envelope. I braced myself, holding my breath as I took it from her. As far as I could rewind memories in my head, I could not replay one of John ever looking so peaceful. It looked as if he were sleeping, his face framed in the alabaster white of a crisp linen bedsheet. The crows' feet that stretched to his temples as he laughed could no longer rival the plushness of his long, dark lashes, and his teeth, never his best feature, were sheltered by well-contoured lips that had previously gone unnoticed, at least by me. It was hard to tear my eyes from him. I was somewhat inclined to slip the photo into my purse. Obviously I didn't envision it framed on my night table, but it offered a cool tranquility that I never wanted to forget.

"There isn't a mark on his face," the examiner offered warmly, as if she couldn't believe it herself.

I was truly torn at this point. I so wanted to be with him, but I didn't know if I could handle it. I slid my fingers along the fold in the newspaper, still on my lap, placing my hand for a moment halfway down the page, holding it where I imagined John's hand had held it just a few hours earlier. "Do you think it would be okay if I held his hand?" I asked, hardly believing the words had come out of my mouth.

Detective Clarke and Officer Nichols exchanged looks, each trying to read what the other's face had to offer. Although they hadn't looked her way yet, the medical examiner said, "I think she'll be okay. The draping is nice and clean."

I appreciated that she didn't skirt the issue or use terminology that I couldn't understand. She and Detective Clarke walked me back to where John lay. I closed my eyes as we approached him, Detective Clarke never letting go of my arm. I heard the examiner lift the sheet, and before I knew it my hand was placed on John's. The skin on top was soft and cool, and I slid my four fingers around to his palm, pressing the top of his hand with my thumb. I didn't think about the condition of his remains. I thought about his presence in my life, and I thanked him for everything, telling him in my head that he would always be a part of me. Of course it was all still surreal, but it felt good to tell him anyway. Looking back, I don't think that I truly believed he was gone. I felt strongly that he could hear every word. I still think he did. I got so oddly relaxed that my hand started to wander up his wrist as I spoke to him. The examiner stopped me then, taking my hand and dropping it gently by my side. Her motion could not have been more tender, but I found it jarring nonetheless. She had broken what felt to be a hypnotic state of mind, and I felt my legs turn to jelly as they led me away.

At some point I must have asked Detective Clarke to contact John's fiancée. It hurts me now to think that I didn't have the courage to contact her myself, but if truth be told, Katherine and I were not exactly close at the time. I cared for her only because John loved her. As close as John and I were, we didn't all hang out a lot. Occasionally my husband and I would go to a concert with them or take in a show. I didn't realize how serious the relationship was until Aunt Celia, prone to shortening names, or worse yet, concocting nicknames without any right of passage, had made the mistake of calling her Kathy. The informal address had happened many times before with girls that John brought over for Sunday evening dinners, but on this occasion Aunt Celia was swiftly and uncharacteristically corrected. "It's Katherine," he said, his eyes meeting Aunt Celia's to make sure she both heard and understood. I was more or less stunned, knowing fully well at that very moment all that such sternness implied. I immediately looked to Brian for his reaction, only to find him more amused than anything else. I told him later that this was the woman John would marry.

And then the proposal came, and it was back up to Aunt Celia's for dinner. Katherine brought her wedding planner in a binder. There were numerous tabs: Bridal Gowns, Bridesmaids' Dresses, Tuxedoes, Flowers, Programs, Honeymoon Resorts. The well-divided sections went on and on as I flipped through them, feigning interest but definitely impressed with her organizational skills. Brian and I joked later with each other that the binder had been prepared years ago, that the only unfinished part was the Groom's Name on the first page. What nerve we had mocking her. If we could have organized the disarray of our own marriage somewhere deep inside Katherine's binder, we would have.

My heart broke for her when I saw her arrive at the medical examiner's office. There are many things that I do not remember about that day, but I clearly remember all the love and support I found in her embrace. She was three weeks from her wedding day. She was the love of John's life. And she was suddenly my lifeline to John in so many ways. We could never have foreseen a bond that could rival the strength of a steel beam. We didn't say much to each other, and I don't recall being at the medical examiner's for much longer. She wanted me to go with her and her sister, but I said I had to go home. I kept thinking about my bed and how I could drown my sorrows in my pillow, how a good, private sob would do me the world of good. She looked concerned, but I assured her that I would be okay.

And I did just that. I went home, escorted by Detective Clarke. I got the feeling that he would have been happier if I had gone with Katherine. I remember likening him to a ventriloquist who needed a more willing partner, only he was too polite to complain about how difficult I was to manipulate. He handed me his card and told me to call him whenever I needed to talk, but he assured me that he would be in touch in the morning. I had no trouble believing him.

The elevator climbed to what I hoped would be my haven in the sky. I leaned the full weight of my body on the door as I closed it behind me, taking in the cluttered room that was my studio-apartment home. The stockings, drooped over the back of the computer chair, were a plummeting reminder of how I thought getting dressed that morning would be the day's greatest challenge. I remember lighting some candles, an effort in vain to bring some warmth to the room. I turned to the answering machine, not wanting to talk to anyone but hoping to hear a voice. There were five messages, all of them from Jules, variations of "Please call me," and "Are you okay?" I remember pacing the room a bit before realizing that it was okay to lie down now. *I'm home. It's okay.* At some point I buried my whole head in a down pillow and drifted off. The sound of the elevator door in the hall woke me abruptly, and I ran to the peephole, thinking somehow it was John. The hall, which seemed a thousand miles away through the distorted glass of the peephole, was long, dark, and narrow, but I could still make out the silhouetted waddle of Mrs. Bertelsman, blood still running through her body, air still moving in and out of her ninety-four-year-old lungs.

Chapter 3

Living

In the days after John's death, I would speak about him in present and past tense, interchangeably. Going from *is* to *was* was a huge adjustment, and then at some point in time, months or years later, everything becomes *the before* and *the after*. Brian and I separated *before* John died. The divorce came through *after* John died. Katherine got her MBA *before* John died. Julie took the leap and bought the Prada boots *after* John died, declaring "Life is short, after all."

I thought a lot about the indeterminable act of living. Somewhere in the first week after John died I stepped off a curb and into the path of an oncoming bus on Third Avenue. It wasn't intentional, but it did occur to me that I thought I didn't have as much to lose as I did just a week before. All of a sudden I was traveling in a vacuum. I felt like I stuck out like a sore thumb, only no one seemed to notice. The bus driver certainly didn't. My act warranted an obnoxious honk, and he gave me one. Would he feel bad if he knew about John?

I went back to work two weeks later, looking forward to a routine and thinking I would find peace there. Cards, small plants, and well-preserved comfort foods decorated my desk. I shut the door and read each note, grateful for every word. Every kind gesture seemed to shed a whole new light on humanity and the beauty of the world. Everyone seemed to want to remember John and to acknowledge my loss. At first I felt the backing of a small society, but with each passing day a member would become disconnected. There were no hostile departures. One by one, they would just quietly slip away.

After the initial outpouring of sympathy, it seemed no one at work knew what to say, and I didn't know what I wanted them to say. I did know that I wanted to talk about how wonderful John was, but it seemed to make people uneasy. So I stopped talking about him, only bringing him up when there was a smooth segue, when one couldn't help but see the strong connection between the topic and the John story I had to share. People who didn't know John still seemed to have trouble with it though. In the beginning there were some gracious queries about John's personality. Then, much to my astonishment, the need for any sort of reverence dissipated. Without missing a beat, one would ask another if they had seen *The West Wing* the night before. I could always tolerate uneasiness in the wake of a John story— that couldn't be helped—but indifference killed me.

So I kept to myself a lot, at least at work. It was easier that way. The evenings were less lonely. Most evenings my posterior was planted on an Upper East Side barstool. It was the type of lifestyle that could easily make a bad situation worse if it weren't for the company of Katherine and Julie. Yes, that's right, Julie. Many a night I had to stop myself from doing a double take in the midst of a John story, struck by the fact that in my darkest hour Julie Murphy is the one who is listening. Here she was, shallow, materialistic Julie, listening. Not scoping the room for good-looking men. Listening. I came to realize that in the aftermath of tragedy those who are there for you will surprise you.

John's friends came out in the evenings too. Many of them we didn't know before John's death. Some were work associates, others old school friends. Everyone had "a John story" to tell, as we called them.

Summer turned into fall quickly that year. I remember opening my office door somewhere around Thanksgiving, not knowing where the months had gone, the sound of laughter wafting in as freely as the scent of fresh-baked pumpkin pie. The merriment of the holiday season had begun, and there was no holding anyone back now. It wasn't that I didn't want everyone to have their fun. It was that their jovial spirits seemed to intensify my isolation. One good-hearted soul was brave enough to attempt cracking my melancholy at the office Christmas party, saying sympathetically, "We're all just here for a short time, Ellen." I raised a glass in dramatic form, toasting the group with, "A Merry Christmas to all, and to all a good night." I took a sip, threw my scarf over my shoulder, and left, unsure why there was such a need to be a drama queen.

I thought a lot throughout the winter about how long one should mourn, knowing fully well that there's no answer to that. It still seemed important to think about it though. I didn't want to become self-indulgent in my grief. It was hard to know when to start making a concerted effort "to move on," as a few well-intentioned people referred to it. What exactly does "moving on" mean, I wondered. It's something people say all the time, but does anyone really know how to do it? I wished people would get more specific with their advice. *Moving on* to me simply meant the passage of time. It wasn't exactly something I could control. And time did keep marching on.

In the spring I flew to Chicago for the American Library Association conference. It was the first time I left New York since John died. A whole year had passed. I remember walking down the corridor at the airport, admiring the throngs of people who were "moving on" at a rapid pace, when out of the masses a tall, suited figure approached me. "You're the mystery sibling," he said in amazed disbelief.

"Excuse me?" I replied, puzzled by the labeling.

"You're John Bannister's sister," he said, smiling broadly, his hand extended to shake mine.

"Yes, I am," I said, not knowing how to react. "I'm Ellen."

"I'm Miles Kastner. I had the pleasure of working with John a few years back. I met you briefly at the wake, and of course I remember you from the funeral," he said, his voice trailing off, not knowing what to say next.

I felt bad for him. He seemed so truly happy to see me, and then neither one of us knew exactly what to say. I didn't want him to regret approaching me. It was as if he hadn't considered the awkward consequences before he greeted me, and for this I was grateful.

"Where did you work with John?" I asked quickly, desperate to stop the wave of regret that appeared to be washing over him.

"We were at Johnson Warner together, before John moved on to Fitz Fuller."

I knew the company names well. I knew the avenues and the cross streets of the buildings that housed the employees of these powerhouses from nine to five, and six, and seven o'clock, and often later than that. It made me sad to think that John worked so hard during a life that was so short, but I had to remind myself how much he seemed to enjoy it all.

Miles and I were quickly slipping into precisely the type of idle chit-chat I could remember teasing John about years earlier. I can remember the two of us running into a former coworker of his on East 86th Street, and I listened as the two of them shared the news of the industry … where they were currently working, what company so-and-so had gone to, and on and on. If it weren't for the genuine warmth of the greeting, the obvious pleasure the chance reunion had brought to both of them, I would have easily become nauseated. Even so, there was much to poke fun at.

"Have you ever noticed," I asked John as we rode the train downtown afterward, "how many of the companies you and your friend have pledged allegiance to that bear two-name titles?" Clearly deep in thought about his conversation with an old friend, he shot me a puzzled look. "I mean Johnson Warner, Fitz Fuller, Brennan and Breen, Long & Long, Baker and Scott," I continued, "they all have two names. It's like a prerequisite for self-importance, for instant success, isn't it?"

His face broke into a smile, and he began to laugh heartily. "Ahhhh, don't start with me, Ellen." The train halted to a stop, and I rose to leave. He pushed his way to the door after me, calling out to me, "El, just remember that we're all good hearts behind the company names, good, hardworking souls, at least most of us."

"I'll try to remember that," I yelled back.

"You do that," he said, waving his finger at me. And then, right before the doors closed on his pointer, he managed to squeeze in, "And I'll have my people call your people." I remember laughing out loud as I walked down the platform, oblivious to anyone who may have noticed. It was like that when you were close with someone. You didn't worry so much about looking foolish.

Miles was on his way to San Francisco, and I was headed back to New York. "Time for a drink?" I asked, surprising myself. I asked questions I would never ask, did things I would never do before John died. I longed to know every facet of him now. I couldn't hear enough about him.

Miles checked his watch. "I've got an hour to kill."

Whether they knew it or not, John's friends, colleagues, and acquaintances played a very big part in my "moving on." Their stories brought me enormous comfort. It was fascinating to me how John's exhilarating spirit had affected so many different people, how his life seemed to fuel a momentum of good will.

Once settled at the airport bar, I asked Miles what I couldn't before. "You called me the mystery sibling. Why?"

"That's what we called you," he responded unapologetically, the shrug of his shoulders indicating that he had to consider why before he continued. "For some reason, we always forgot that John had a sister. We all seemed to have it engraved in our heads that he was an only child, and whenever he brought you up, the words *my sister* always seemed new to us. Then we would plague him with questions about you, wanting to know why we hadn't met you, as if he were lying about your existence. It was all very good-natured."

Then, as if suddenly realizing his good-naturedness may have negative consequences, he touched my arm lightly and said, "I hope this doesn't upset you. It's not that he didn't talk about you. We just always forgot."

"Not at all. Quite to the contrary, I'm sort of enjoying this." I didn't mention it to Miles, but my coworkers always forgot about John too. I would start talking about his upcoming wedding or how I needed to pick up his birthday gift, and I would get these blank stares for a second, and then "I always forget you have a brother." It was interesting to hear that John experienced the same sort of reaction.

"Well good, because there was certainly nothing negative about it."

"Nothing negative taken," I assured him.

"Then he would inevitably have to tell us something about you, saying that you didn't like hanging out a lot, that your interests were very different than his own."

"Very true." I didn't want to elaborate on how I was different, so I waited for him to speak again.

"There was a lot of stupid nicknaming going on. Sometimes we couldn't remember how the names originated, but they were used regularly in our conversations anyway. For example, John was The Mayah."

"Oh The Mayor! Yes, I heard of that one," I said with glee.

Miles quickly corrected me, swaying his finger back and forth like an upside down pendulum. "Not The May*or*, The May*ah*. Ya' gotta remember that some of these boys were from the Boston area, and that's how the name went down, *The Mayah*. You know why, right?"

"Go 'head," I said, throwing my head back a bit, welcoming his rendition, not wanting to taint it with what I had already heard.

"Wherever we went with him, he knew somebody. It didn't matter where we were. Uptown, Downtown, SoHo, Tribeca, Queens, Harlem, you name it, he ran in to someone he knew. And he was always so happy to see them. It was as if he knew each one intimately too, and ya had to wonder how the hell someone like him knew all these people. How did he ever have the time to get to know all these people? Now, I pride myself on knowing a lot of people, and remembering a lot of names too, but this level of interaction, and with such frequency, none of us understood. And there was never any hesitation. Ya know how you would see someone coming, and maybe ya hadn't seen them in a while, and the panic would flush over you? Do I say hello or don't I?" Miles took too big a swig from his beer and wiped the excess with the back of his hand. "It always seemed as if that never happened to him. It was like that fear never gripped him. And so we took to calling him The Mayah, for those obvious reasons. The only part of the name that didn't ring true was that he never bullshitted people, like a mayor would."

Although there was nothing sentimental about the way Miles spoke—actually, he had a very matter-of-fact way about him— my eyes began to tear a bit, because John really was that person.

□

That evening, back in New York, I called one of John's dearest friends, Tony. I didn't know Tony before John died, but he was one of two people I sought after the funeral. His name kept echoing in my head, and it was all because of one night at Aunt Celia's when John came in and laid his cell phone on the table, as if he would be paying homage to it. He never said it, but we knew this meant that he would be taking a call, mid meal or not. I rarely saw him on his cell phone, so its presence on the table definitely sparked my curiosity. It even piqued Uncle Ed's interest. Dulled from years of having little opportunity to talk, there wasn't much that stimulated him anymore. We just sat there, eating quietly, waiting for it to ring, the anticipation building with every bite. The silence proved to be unbearable for Aunt Celia, who left the table at one point to retrieve a single plate from the kitchen. I don't think any of us thought much about what she was doing until she slammed the plate down in front of an empty chair and placed the phone on it. "For whoever will be joining us," she said theatrically.

"All right," John said, his hand up to protect himself. In an effort to placate her, he was about to share everything when the phone rang. Before Aunt Celia could protest, he swiftly grabbed the phone and left the room. I could still hear him though. "Why not?" he asked, struggling to control his temper.

He returned to the room crestfallen, and though he didn't feel like it, he had to tell us all about it. "I've been on my high school's alumni board for several years, and I, along with countless others, recommended that this guy Tony Orslany be promoted to Director of Advancement, a role that should have been a natural next step for him. He had already served in various administrative and directorial positions at the school for years, and now that the position of Director of Advancement was open they had to decide whether to promote from within or hire from the outside. Needless to say, they chose the latter."

After a long silence, John spoke at length about Tony's many attributes, but primarily about his passion for building strong relationships, "a crucial skill for the job." What was a quiet tribute eventually turned bitter. "I'm tired of good people being overlooked. Tony had only one thing working against him ... he's competent. If he were incompetent, the job would be his. Positions of authority are reserved for only the most incompetent people." John rarely made statements without logical backing, and he was letting his raw emotions do the talking, but it was precisely his bitterness and deep disillusionment that made me remember Tony.

Sometimes it is the most unusual names that stick with you. If it had been Smith or Miller I may not have remembered it, but Orslany stuck with me. It not only stuck with me, I could hear John saying it in my head. Knowing that Tony had so many qualities that John admired, I sought him out after John's passing, not knowing that it would lead to one of the most meaningful friendships of my life.

Tony knew all the people John hung out with over the years, so naturally I had to call him after running into Miles. Throughout that first year we always touched base whenever we heard something new. I didn't tell him about my chance encounter at first. I just asked if he was available to have dinner at Triumph, a local stomping ground, a place John had frequented. Katherine and Jules came too. After the waitress took the menus, I launched into the story. "Does the name *Miles Kastner* mean anything to you?"

"Miles Kastner," Tony repeated as he relaxed into the back of the chair.

"Oh that idiot Miles," Katherine chimed in.

"He was one of the guys from Johnson Warner," Tony said reflectively. "He wasn't such a bad guy, was he?"

"I always thought he was a little crass," Katherine said.

"He told me I was the mystery sibling, a.k.a. the forgotten sister."

"Uh, the mystery sibling," Tony exhaled.

"You knew about that and never told me?"

"I actually forgot about it. By the way, John hated that they called you that."

"He did?" I asked, bewildered at first. "I sort of like that they gave me a nickname."

"Well, think about it. If you had only one sibling, and the same people kept forgetting that that sibling existed, wouldn't it piss you off too? When you care about someone as much as John cared about you, it would piss you off."

Tony said nothing that I didn't already know. I knew John loved me. Still, all the same, it was really nice to hear someone I know John admired telling me as much. It's silly, but the confirmation of it all brought tears to my eyes. I was so fortunate to have Tony. I really felt that John led me to him. It was a strong pull that I felt, and whenever I was with him I felt comfort and I felt John's quintessential goodness.

Pain cannot be measured, but I sensed that Tony took John's death hard, and his pain absorbed some of mine. I hoped that I took some of his hit too. I still hope I do today, four years later. But something funny happened toward the end of that first year. I began to realize that the tragedy that bonded us did not define us. We were, and we still are, two people traveling in different directions. The beauty of it all is that we altered our paths so that we could be there for each other when we needed to be. There can be great beauty in grief, and my bond with Tony is an example of it.

It wasn't lost on me that John's favorite song, a song he and I had spoken about many times, began playing as we finished our dinner that night at the corner table in Triumph. It was fun to discuss meeting Miles, but my thoughts kept going back to the one other person I felt I should meet, a fellow by the name of Birchie. I wondered that very night at Triumph how it could be that I still had not met this man. Tony or Katherine mentioned once or twice that he had been at the funeral, but neither one stayed in contact with him. I didn't realize back then that his would be a name I would keep hearing John say in my head. I had been wondering about Birchie for a whole year. He unwittingly taunted me.

There had actually been a glimmer of Birchie one autumn evening, just months after John's death, when Tony suddenly put his drink down on the bar one night and started pointing up at the television screen in disbelief at the exact moment my eyes were focusing on the name *Chris Birchovsky.* Inexplicably, I had just been sitting there, wondering why I hadn't met Birchie yet, and there he was, in some downtown bar being interviewed about the outcome of the World Series. "That's Birchie," Tony said, rising to get a good look.

I took Birchie in as much as I could, frantic that the camera would fan to the next person all too soon, but I saw plenty of Birchie. He was large, round, red-faced, and somewhat disheveled. And while I couldn't hear what he was saying, there was something quite vulgar about the way he kept pointing into the camera, his gyrations causing his beer to spill. His crudeness aside, there was something mystical about seeing him on television at that given moment. I had been having these experiences that felt like quick pulses of energy, and they always climaxed in an occurrence that was simply unbelievable. I thought about him and he sort of appeared, but then he slipped into the deep, dark abyss again.

Many people call these occurrences coincidences. Skeptics would say that I was looking for signs to comfort me. I probably would have agreed, only it was so strange living through them. Besides, if I were merely looking for comfort I would have to argue that there was nothing comforting about the sight of Birchie.

☐

The worst of times were followed by the best of times, and sometimes it seemed that the two occurred simultaneously. In many ways the aftermath of John's death was a magical period,

29

one I knew would eventually pass. I don't know how I knew, but I was quite sure of it. I can remember talking to John in my head, thanking him for being with me, knowing that he had to go soon, that he couldn't comfort me in a multitude of ways anymore, telling him I know he'll always be with me. We were all celebrating the life of someone we loved, and none of us wanted that to end, but something was beginning to happen. We weren't seeing as much of each other anymore.

Chapter 4

Cycles

I have been around long enough to know that the ups and downs of publishing come in cycles, and we at Burke & Patterson were riding a downward spoke. When optimistic forecasts were not met, there was always a strong inclination on the part of the hierarchy to take something that was successful in the past and thinly reinvent it. I couldn't help but remind the powers that be, as I presented them with a folder that highlighted the poor sales of long-dead horses, that these spin-off ideas never seemed to do well for us. The folder lay there in the middle of the conference table, like a small, unwanted boat that had gone adrift on a sea of mahogany. Four years after John's death, and I, too, was sick of thinly reinventing myself. I longed for freshness in every compartment of my life.

A few seconds of utter silence elapsed, and then, in an effort to summon as much attention as possible, my immediate boss—I have many of them—cleared his throat, which I always considered a sign of impending doom. I looked up in time to see his eyes dart from side to side as he said, with great pomp and circumstance, "I've been saving this one for a rainy day." His top lip bore down heavily over his bottom lip, and a sense of dread came over me.

Elliot wasn't exactly a bad fellow. We just didn't see eye-to-eye on many things. "The problem with you, Ellen," he would say, with condescending admiration, "is that you never see the bottom line clearly."

It wasn't long before we were paraded out to the main reception area, a large marble foyer that accommodated the elevator bank on one side and a tribute wall to our best-selling authors on the other. The wall was Burke & Patterson's version of Grauman's Chinese Theatre, only there had been several time capsules implanted in it twenty years earlier that contained the hopes and aspirations, and perhaps the occasional first draft of what had become a wildly successful book, of those who were thought to become the company's future literary icons. The installment of the time capsules had generated much favorable publicity for the company at the time and had resulted in a temporary, but significant, boost in sales. Photographs of the day still decorate the reception area and line the halls, spawning a barrage of inquiries from guests and new employees alike. In fact, one of Julie's catch-all responsibilities was to hand out printed information packets to those with questions. And now I could see her, out of the corner of my eye, eagerly setting aside whatever she was doing so that she could position herself for one of the many high-drama performances she had grown accustomed to at Burke & Patterson over the years. Her chin fell into the shock-resistant web of her interlocked fingers, and she waited while we positioned ourselves around Elliot. I swear these spontaneous moments are what kept her at the company. I often thought there was so much more she could be doing with her life. But who am I to say?

Elliot's hands went up like those of a conductor's, pointing in this direction and that, dictating how several more authors could be added to the wall here and there. To my horror, it was also part of his plan to move some of the time capsules to another location to make room for new additions. "For example, Dorothea Fredericks's doesn't need to be here anymore," he declared. I looked to the president, Elliot's boss, to gauge his reaction. There was a composed nod, indicating that he wanted to hear more.

If our tribute wall could be compared to Grauman's Chinese Theatre, then Dorothea Fredericks was our Greta Garbo, only she became a recluse far sooner than Garbo. Her first novel sold five million copies in its first year, and instant fame quickly overtook her. It was just one of those flukes. She never saw it coming. No one did. And now no one but Julie knew that I was fortunate enough to get to know her through phone conversations over the years, and I greatly admired her. Her editor retired several years before I joined the company, and apparently she had been bounced around from person to person whenever she needed to order more copies of her book.

My first conversation with her was quite brief and rather humdrum. In fact, she was long forgotten by the time I waited for the elevator at lunchtime. "She asked for someone with a heart," Julie said, while I hummed a tune. I looked around to see no one else in the reception area.

"Hmmm?" was all I could think to say.

"Dorothea Fredericks. She asked for someone with a heart. So I transferred her to you."

I could feel an unexpected smile spread across my face. "Nice to hear I still have a heart, Jules."

If Dorothea Fredericks ever needed anything, I was more or less there for her. Her requests were always simple, and the timeless stories that came with them erased the years between us. She had a way of tapping into the most basic human sensations, the things that never changed, emotions that everyone experienced but many didn't feel comfortable acknowledging. And that was just it. She was comfortable with herself, and she left the public eye so that she could remain so. That was my take on her. But in the eyes of those who sit on plush swivel chairs at Burke & Patterson, she could have done so much more for the company before choosing to become a recluse.

Much to my surprise, I found my arm going up to get Elliot's attention.

"Yes, Ellen?" he said zealously, as if he were a mentor and I his ever-eager pupil. He was always willing to hear what I had to say. I'll give him that.

"Isn't it usually understood that once a time capsule is put in place it is to remain in that place for a specified period of time, all of these being twenty-five years?" I asked.

He looked at me blankly, as if I had spoken a foreign language. I continued on, struggling to find the words that would spark some kind of recognition, something that might result in "Aha! I knew someone was going to raise that point!"

"I mean, I guess I'm worried about the public's trust, not to mention our own integrity," I persisted. At this he grew a little more thoughtful, as if considering our image for the first time.

"I see what you're saying, Ellen, but I really think there are several names here that simply wouldn't be missed. And even if we do get a bit of backlash, the attention the newer names will draw, the subsequent revenue such publicity could generate, will surely make it worth our while."

A few heads in the group started to bobble up and down, some halfheartedly at first. There was really only one thing left to do at this point. "Dorothea Fredericks," I said, hoping I resonated enough over voices that were beginning to buzz with a contagious enthusiasm. The momentum died down for a second, and I repeated her name for effect before I continued. "Dorothea Fredericks. There is something about a recluse such as Fredericks. Her mystique will only fuel curiosity over time. I think it would be a huge mistake to move her, particularly when she already has a strong following." Elliot had a pained look on his face, as if he were struggling with the notion that anyone could have interest in Dorothea Fredericks.

"Isn't that right, Julie?" I asked.

Julie's hands quickly fell away from her chin. "I'm sorry, what was that?" I saw her hands working swiftly, and she managed to hold up a single sheet of paper by the time most eyes were on her. "I'm sorry. I wasn't listening. I was busy reading. What was that?"

"People ask where Dorothea Fredericks's capsule is all the time, right?"

"Oh absolutely."

"That's really quite interesting," Elliot conceded. "Julie, I'd love to hear more about interest in the wall, and who better to hear it from than you."

I knew I would take the heat for that one later from Julie, but I had to pull out whatever stops I could for Dorothea Fredericks. Reluctant to hear much more, I slipped away before the group disbanded. On the way back to my office I paused at the photograph taken of Fredericks twenty years earlier. She looked like a small deer caught in the headlights as she stood to the left of the gold-engraved letters that formed her name. The mausoleum-like block proved to be somewhat of a professional death sentence. One year folded into another, and still there was no second book. As much as any of us knew, she never wrote again.

As I turned to continue down the hall, I held back for a second to examine my own reflection in the glass. I was roughly the same age as Fredericks was in the picture. I was okay looking, and nothing more. My hair, curly and a common mousy brown, was bound tight in its usual pony tail. My eyes, in pictures and now in the reflection, were as hollow and inanimate as beads on a stuffed bunny. While my features were pleasant enough to render me mildly attractive, heads didn't turn in the street. I was content to go unnoticed most of the time, but there were those fleeting moments when I wished that something would cause my eyes to shine with an intensity seen in those of Fredericks, even if it was the result of uneasiness. At least she once reached outside herself. At least she really lived.

As I entered my office the sun hit the waxy texture of an envelope on my desk long enough to cause it to gleam for a fraction of a second. As I made my way around the desk something old yet new stirred inside me. For weeks I had eagerly flipped through the daily mail in search of another letter, as if a brown waxy envelope somehow held the key to myself. Then one day I forced myself to stop looking. And now here it was, not weeks but months after the first one had arrived. There was something shameful in my quiet excitement. Why, I asked, had I allowed myself to want another letter from a complete stranger? And again, no return address. Why had I let this person mess with my head? I picked up my letter opener as if it were a sword that had won me many battles and sliced into the envelope.

Dear Ellen:

It is late autumn, and I am tired. My hips ache from bending to pick up apples that have rotted on the ground. The nip in the air doesn't help, but still I am grateful to have the opportunity to do something I have always done, even if it does hurt in ways it never did before. I will keep doing it as long as I can, mainly because routine has grown increasingly important to me with age. It is a way I measure my physical well-being, and perhaps my own longevity. This increased activity has led me in and out of the barn with greater frequency than usual. Occasionally I will stop to rest, and to contemplate. The motorcycle, the means which created the path to my daughter's demise, lies propped against the wooden planks that my grandfather nailed in place long before my father was born. I wonder sometimes if my father and grandfather thought much about legacy, if it occurred to them that sometimes one's legacy is cut short. I'm sure it did. I'm sure every parent worries about losing a child. My advice to them: Don't dwell on it for long. Chances are that you will long be gone, and hopefully, that you will be waiting somewhere peaceful for your children to join you. Besides, a life cannot be lived well if it is gripped with fear for long. Fear is normal, and even healthy, but I am a firm believer that one must overcome it if it serves no positive purpose. I used to kick the front wheel in anger, but now I know that if this bike can be fixed, I will ride it. I will lift the cover and stare every inch of it down. Come spring I will ride it.

Clem

I put the letter down and agonized over it, as I knew I would before I slit the envelope. Then I opened my desk drawer and pulled out the letter from months earlier to compare the postmarks. Then I did something I never did before. I called a car rental service.

Chapter 5

The Beginning of a Journey

Although it wasn't much more than an hour's drive from Manhattan, Cider Banks, New York, might as well have been on the other side of the planet to me. Julie didn't like what I was doing, but she nonetheless introduced me to Mapquest, an internet creation for which many New Yorkers without cars have little need. We plugged in the address of a Cider Banks business to give me a general sense of where I was going, and then there was little else to do but wait for Saturday morning.

With Saturday morning came pouring rain and belly-aching dread. I didn't plan on staying overnight, but I had a small duffle bag packed by 5 a.m. just in case. I nursed two cups of coffee by the window, watching the sky go from jet to gray, and then I e-mailed Brian nothing more than *Going to Cider Banks for a day or two. Be back in touch on Sunday.* It sounded nice, *Going to Cider Banks,* even whimsical, like it was a happy occasion. I had always been direct with Brian, and I wondered if he would think my coyness odd. It was easy to envision him tilting back in his chair and saying, *Okay, I get it. You found someone. Big deal! Fill me in.* But I couldn't tell him what I didn't understand. I hadn't much of a clue why I was taking this journey. Was it curiosity? Maybe some. Mostly it was something else, something that came as naturally as breathing to some but was difficult for me. I had something I needed to overcome. I found it hard to take big chances. Something always held me back. Perhaps a skittish nature. Some have it, some don't. If I started to talk like this to Brian, he would worry. Although we didn't move each other in mysterious ways anymore, we were good friends. Everyone should be so lucky to have a Brian in life. Letting go was the best thing we could have done for each other.

All along there have been many things that I've tried to dismiss in life, but try as I might I could not get this 78-year-old man out of my head. If I could have let go of it, I would have. I thought a lot about letting go while I filled out the necessary paperwork at the garage, droplets from my wet hair causing the blue ink to smudge. I knew in some way this trip was very much about letting go, although I couldn't find the words to explain it beyond that. It involved letting go and holding on at the same time, and I knew that there was something about it that was meant to honor John. It was out of character for me to do this, and John was always trying to get me to reach inside myself, as if I could find something that I didn't know was there, as if a weight could suddenly be lifted off my chest and I could breathe as easily as he could. "People are different," I would tell him. "We're not all like you."

"Ma'am, your car is here." I was relieved to find an inconspicuous gray sedan awaiting me. The young attendant hopped out and held the door open for me. "I'd be happy to put that in the trunk for you," he said, motioning to my duffle bag.

"Thank you, but that's all right. I'll keep it up front with me." There were things in it I wanted near me. My cell phone, for one, but perhaps even dearer to me was a photograph of me, John, and the man who had graded my road test when I applied for a driver's license, a man whose name I'm not sure I ever knew. The photograph was there for the sake of good karma. It had been years since I had driven a car, and I needed to believe that it was as easy as getting back on a bike, which I'm not sure is as easy as people say it is. The thought of the photograph calmed my nerves as I made my way up the FDR Drive. I was careful to choose the middle lane to create a buffer zone for myself, a pointer I had learned years earlier from my driving instructor. The FDR led me to The Major Deegan Expressway, a route that eventually turns into The New York State Thruway. As bricks and concrete gave way to foliage, I could feel my grip—on 10 and 2, of course—begin to relax. A release was coming over me, and I let my mind rewind to the weeks leading up to the day the photograph was taken.

On a rare outing to Jones Beach one hot summer day, John had pestered Brian and me to reveal what our "attainable" dreams were. Neither one of us had wished to partake in the conversation. I was in the middle of a good book, and Brian preferred snoozing to talking. Nonetheless, John persuaded us to postpone our chosen pleasures for ten minutes to pursue a conversation that could "potentially yield long-term gratification for both of us," as he put it, looking at me slyly out of the corner of his eye as he maneuvered his rental onto the Long Island Expressway. He knew I abhorred finance talk, and he waited his own obligatory five seconds before bursting into a hearty chuckle. With some reluctance, I folded the book over my arm so as not to lose my place.

Brian's rapid response interrupted my thoughts. "Archery," he said.

I looked around quickly, thinking I must not have heard him correctly.

"Come again?" John asked patiently.

"Archery. I wouldn't mind having some skill with a bow and arrow."

"What on earth for?" I asked in disbelief.

"It just might be kind of neat. That's all."

I was still looking at him when his head fell back, his eyes already closed.

"You know that couldn't have been more insincere, right?" I asked John. "He just wants to sleep."

"Nevermind that. It's your turn."

As I watched John change lanes, I said, "I might want to learn how to drive someday. I mean, I don't need to know right now, but maybe someday I will."

That September John presented Brian with a birthday certificate for five archery lessons at a Lower East Side establishment called Bull's Eye. "Uhm, thanks man," Brian said, somewhat perplexed, clearly not remembering his attainable dream. I could feel my mouth contorting into a smirk, so I thought it was a good time to clear the cake plates from the table. John was quick on my heels into the kitchen.

"I have a little something for you too, El," he said.

"Really? What's the occasion?"

"Let's just say an early birthday gift."

I looked at him like he was stretching a truth.

"Okay, a REALLY early birthday gift." He slid a driver's permit exam booklet across the counter to me, along with a certificate for five driving lessons. "Why can't someday be today?"

"But I have no need to learn how to drive right now."

"That doesn't matter. It's something you want to do. Right?" I looked up from the booklet. "I'll go with you," he said.

And he did. We both knew the permit test wouldn't be a problem. Even so, he gave me a 10 p.m. quiz by phone every night for a week. Then he came to three of the driving lessons, which were terrifying. As a stalling tactic during parallel parking practice, I kept blaming my forgetfulness on him, even though he said little, if anything, from the backseat. "Maybe it would be better if he weren't in the car," I said to the instructor on one occasion.

"Your call," the instructor had said, his mouth curling into a smile.

Then John opened the door to climb out. "No, don't leave," I said. Then he lifted his foot back into the car. "No, do." The foot went back out, this time like it was independent of his body, and he was no longer waiting for my instructions. He had started snapping his fingers and was performing his own one-footed tap dance that came with singing: "Ah, fly me to the moon, and let me play among the stars. Let me know what life is like on Jupiter and Mars." And though I knew he had jeans and a sweater on, when I relive it in my head he dons a tux.

And of course he came to the road tests. I say *tests* because I failed the first time. The second time he had stood at the curb like an expectant father. I pulled up ever so slowly, aligning the car with where he stood. I put the gear stick in park and exhaled, turning my head slowly to find him. His hands, two tight fists, were forced into the front pockets of his blue jeans, and although he stood about six feet tall upright, he was more than willing to crouch to half his size for early results. "She pass?" he had whispered.

He later claimed that he had no doubt that I would, hence the camera. I was grateful he hadn't told me about it. I started jumping up and down with glee when he pulled it out. "You're just lucky I didn't see that thing. You know I would have caved under the pressure if I saw that thing," I yelled at him, laughing and throwing my finger in his face like a giddy fool.

He had a way of corralling me before my geek factor kicked in full force. "All right, all right, calm down," he said, motioning to my clipboard-clad test giver to join us. The reserved soul looked confused at first. "Time for a group photo," John had explained.

"Oh sure," he said, approaching us with his hand out.

"No, no, we need you in it," John said.

"Uhm, how 'bout I just take one of the two of you," he responded uneasily. Of course John would hear none of it, and he quickly summoned a passerby to capture the moment.

Then he drove me uptown. I can still hear him in my head. "Look, I gotta return the car to Egan. Where should I let you out?"

"At D'Agostino's is good." The lightness to my mood had brought on a craving for a juicy steak dinner, maybe a little red wine. I punched him lightly in the arm as he steered his way to the curb. "Anybody ever tell you you're all right, John boy?" Then my silliness gave way to a sentimental sensation. I felt I owed him more than that, and I hooked him around the neck with my arm. "Seriously, John. Thank you. That was an awesome gift."

I was surprised to feel the weight of his hand in the crook of my elbow as I turned to leave. He waited for me to turn around before speaking, and then he looked me dead straight in the eyes. "El, you never know when you might want to take a ride. Rent a car. Go away for a weekend. Think things through."

There was an awkward silence, and I could feel my emotions rising to the surface. There was no point in holding them back. He could always see right through me anyway. "I know," I whispered, the tears beginning to pool in the corners of my eyes, embarrassment burning my face. We had never talked about it, but I knew what he meant. It was a reference to life as I knew it, with Brian. He could see that we weren't happy together, and he wanted me to do whatever I could to be happy again. To John, it really was that simple. He was never one to accept a stagnant, halfhearted relationship, and I know my union with Brian puzzled him. It was never enough for John to be merely comfortable, and there was no point in trying to explain that comfort is enough for some. The argument would fall on deaf ears. Besides, I wasn't strong enough yet to realize that comfort wasn't enough for me either. So I would remain deaf too.

"I'm sorry," he had said, kissing me on the forehead. "Just know I'm here for you, whatever you do."

☐

A runny nose and streaks of moisture on my cheeks aroused me from what can only be described as a meditative state. I was so oddly relaxed until I remembered the mission I was on. Then I could feel the morning's coffee curdling in my stomach. *Yep, there's that old familiar feeling. There's the anxiety that forms your very existence. Welcome back, Ellen Bannister.*

Chapter 6

A Rehearsed Performance

Julie, knowing that I was not prepared to tell Clem who I was, had warned me to reinvent myself. "Be prepared to lie," she had said, "but stay as close to the truth as you can." It had occurred to me as I listened to her that deception, for some, was a well-studied art form, and that typing and proofreading were just part of her repertoire of proficiencies. Finely honed skills were likely to be as endless as the contents of her black leather shoulder bag.

"You obviously don't want to say you're an editor," she had said. "Let's see ... something in the book business though." The tapping of her well-manicured fingernail, a mild annoyance to me, proved to be inspirational. "I've got it! Tell him you're a librarian and that you've been toying with the idea of writing a book on apple farming. You know, as a bit of a hobby. Nothing too technical, but something very visual ... for God's sake, you don't want to have to listen to him drone on and on about the science of it all ... a coffee-table book," she said, pleased with herself.

I rehearsed the story many times in my head as I made my way through the small but vibrant village of Cider Banks, "New York's Little Apple," population 3,000. It was mid morning, and the rain was just beginning to taper. Umbrellas of every color bobbed cheerfully along the narrow sidewalks that bordered Main Street. Some were folded early in polite gestures to make room, others in an optimistic confidence that seemed to reflect the locale.

It was clear that the rain had delayed a flurry of Saturday morning errands, but in spite of what must have seemed like pedestrian traffic in such a small community, the residents of Cider Banks were still able to perform a graceful weave in and out of stores, cordially greeting this one and that one along the way. It was like I was watching a scene in an old movie. These people knew each other. Any minute now Jimmy Stewart would tip his hat, but it wouldn't be in my direction. It was oddly intimidating, even from the shelter of the car. The only good thing about such intimacy was that I would surely find someone who knew an apple farmer named Clem. The bad part, I may have to pay dearly for the information. Inquiring minds would want to know who I was or what business I had with him.

Set back from the road about halfway through the village stood an intriguing stone structure that would have passed for comfortable lodging at any Revolutionary War encampment. Upon closer inspection I realized that it now functioned as the Cider Banks Post Office. I pulled the car into the lot and took a deep breath, reassuring myself once again that I had nothing to be ashamed of here. I had a right to be here. He wrote to me, for God's sake! A voyeuristic psychopath I am not.

The door closing behind me created an echo loud enough to alert anyone who cared that I was in the building. But no one did care. A gentleman to the left kept his back to me, clearly more interested in leafing through the mail he had just pulled from his post-office box. I walked up to the lone window—apparently there was need for only one—and stretched my neck halfheartedly through it, afraid that I would see someone. After reminding myself that that was the point, I rang the small, silver-plated bell, which did elicit a reaction from the back room.

"Be right with you," a female's voice countered cheerfully. A tidy middle-aged woman emerged, her face framed with tight, well-coiffed curls. "What can I do for you?" she asked pleasantly. Her sweet disposition must have bolstered my confidence, because I lied like I didn't know I could. It wasn't even part of the script to lie to her. It just happened, quickly and painlessly. I began to babble like a brook overflowing from the morning's rain.

"Yeah, I was apple picking in the area a few years back, and I just can't seem to catch my bearings. I know it was right around here, and the apple farmer's name was Clem, but I just can't seem ...." I didn't need to go any further. Recognition lit up her face like a 200-watt light bulb.

"Clem Vance," she said eagerly, following it with specific and generous directions, leaning toward me to point this way and that, eventually pulling out a pen and pad to draw a map. Her reaction calmed me. It was the only insight I had into the old man other than the letters, and I thought he couldn't be too bad. As I turned to leave I asked if the farm had a name. "No," she said, still thinking. "You may see a small carved sign, APPLES FOR SALE." Then she smiled. I took the smile to be a subtle tribute to the man's simplicity. And I told myself as I walked out that uncalculated lying is guilt-free.

His farm was off a back road, three miles out of town. While the town itself seemed to be born of woodland, the back road formed a hypnotic passage through gently rolling hills of grass and well-cultivated farmland. The fog hung low over some of the darkest soil I had ever seen, surely rich in something, I thought. On another day it would have been breathtaking, but the business at hand could never escape me for long.

I found the dilapidated sign at the bottom of a long, graveled drive, and I pulled the car onto a shoulder of mossy grass and small pebbles. Any hope that I had come upon the wrong farm was beginning to fade. It was exactly as the woman said it would be. The apple trees formed neat rows to the left of the drive, and although the finer details were veiled in the fog, I could still make out the colonial red barn and the white clapboard farmhouse at the top of the hill.

I took a deep breath and observed as much as I could from behind the steering wheel, but there wasn't much going on. It seemed safe enough to quietly slip out of the car and take a few steps. I had never been in an apple orchard before and was surprised that the trees were so small, the branches so spidery. I held a branch firmly and tugged hard at one of the apples. I immediately felt a presence around me and froze, afraid that any movement would embed me deeper in the web of the tree, but it was already too late to escape.

When I first spotted Clem Vance, he was standing at the top of an incline halfway through the grove. He could have been there a while for all I knew, maybe even before I pulled up, but it felt like he snuck up on me. He knew I saw him and he spoke right away, his breath breaking through the fog. "Go on, take a bite," he hollered. I just kept on looking at him, as if English were a third or fourth language to me. "It's a McCoun," he yelled down patiently. "Best eating apple 'round."

I looked at the fruit's skin thoughtfully. "What about the pesticides?" I yelled up.

He stood there for a minute, his slouching frame a dead giveaway that he had just lost considerable enthusiasm for the conversation. He shuffled downhill anyway, finding his balance with the support of a tree branch here and there. His twill pants and quilted vest, the stitch work of which created diamond-shaped pillows, were riddled with dirt. He was a walking monument to the natural, spotted pigment of wild mushrooms. If it weren't for his sleeves, red-and-black checkerboard flannel, his outline could have easily been lost to the October earth. As he made his way toward me I stood motionless and began to make out the finer details of his face. His skin was weathered, but his eyes expressed a curiosity usually long gone in a man half his age. "Where you from?" he asked, peering at me from under a taupe cap, tufts of snow-white hair emerging from both sides. The softness in his voice made me never want to disappoint him again, but I somehow knew my one-word response would.

"Manhattan," I said.

"Thought so," he said. He held his hand out and said the two words that sealed the deal: "Clem Vance." I took his hand and stood there quietly, as if I had just reached a dead end and there was nowhere else to go. He dropped his head a little lower, concentrating hard so as not to miss anything, and his posture took on a stance that was a mixture of searching and waiting.

My heart skipped a bit at the thought that he might recognize me from somewhere. Then it occurred to me that he was offering me a courtesy that usually warrants an exchange. "El," I said, which was true. "Short for Elizabeth," which was not.

It didn't matter that I didn't know where I was going with the conversation. He did. "Look," he said, his hand held out emphatically, "the pesticides won't kill you. You won't know which apples you fancy unless you try a few. Then you can take the ones you like home and scrub the hell out of 'em. Scrub 'em till your heart's content," he said, a smile playing at the corners of his mouth as he turned to go back in the direction from which he came, muttering a "Jesus Christ" under his breath. As he walked away a loneliness crept back into my chest, and I was relieved when he turned halfway around and said, "Well come on. I have some Cortlands back up this way. We'll figure it all out." I followed him up the hill like a puppy that had just latched onto a kindhearted stranger.

There was no need to perform with him. He didn't seem to care who I was. He welcomed me into his world, no questions asked. He was trusting and free, and his passion for his work was exhilarating. After a short while I was able to look beyond the well-packed soil under his fingernails.

"Do you bake?" he asked.

"No," I said, "but I've always admired the precision of measurement it demands."

"I'll bet you do," he said, giving me a quick once-over. It was only then that I reflected on what I had selected for clothing. I had to acknowledge that I did appear to be wound a little too tight for a rainy day of apple picking. My L. L. Bean driving moccasins were caked with mud, as were my black tights. And although it was nowhere near bitter cold, I wore wool gloves, which I removed every time he offered me another apple. Even so, his critiquing was a little unfair, considering what I had to overlook.

He plucked an Empire and a McIntosh for me, saying "These are great for eating, and they're good for baking too." I bit from the Empire. As he watched me chew he said, "You get that nice crisp snap. It's a great eating apple."

"Hmmmm, that's good," I said, trying to convince him that I truly appreciated it. I was about to bite into the McIntosh when he stopped me.

"Hold on a minute," he said, taking it from me, holding it in the air, his palm creating an altar for worship. "Before you sink your teeth in I just want you to take note of its bright red coat. It's just pretty to look at, isn't it?"

"It sure is," I said, knowing that even if I dived in deep I wouldn't be able to come up with anything more intelligent to say on the matter. It was a little frustrating to be so completely out of my element, not to be able to anticipate his thoughts, not to be able to offer him anywhere near a stimulating conversation. It only mattered to me because I didn't want him to walk off. I suppose life had dealt me a share of male-abandonment issues. My father was gone, and now John. Although they never intentionally left, they were nonetheless gone. And of course, Brian, the one who should have left, was the one who stayed. It was painful to think that this old man, if he chose to, could touch his hand to the brim of his cap, wish me a nice day, and walk back into the fog from which he had emerged. And I was nowhere near ready to yell out, "Why do you write to me?"

He gave the apple back, saying "Go on now," with a welcoming nod. He never watched me eat for long. There was a politeness about him. He would turn to keep climbing, but the tutorial was constant. "It's a versatile apple ... good eating apple ... tenderizes well when cooked ... and it's just nice to look at. And it's great in cobblers."

We made our way through the grove this way, slowly ascending gently cascading mounds of soil with an apple tasting here and there and plenty of small conversation, which seemed to come naturally to him.

"The reason I asked about baking is that my sister runs an afternoon baking class in the house kitchen. Thought you might like to give it a go. For seven dollars she'll provide the ingredients for whatever you want to make and offer her guidance along the way. Best of all, you get to take the fruits of your labor home with you. Now if that ain't a steal I don't know what is."

"Considering how hopeless I am in that area, it's highway robbery."

And then his volley hit me like a ton of bricks. "What *is* your area?" he asked.

I stumbled my way through a response, glad he didn't have eyes at the back of his head, although it felt like he did sometimes. I wondered if he questioned how genuine I was. I said something about being a school librarian who had a dream to write a nature book, maybe even one on apples. "Isn't that funny?" I asked. I was grateful he didn't wait long to hear more.

"Nothing funny about it if that's what you want to do. Never ignore a desire to do something, no matter how silly it seems. I suppose we all have ridiculous thoughts from time to time, but if they stay with you … then that's when you have to pay attention to them."

In the better part of an hour, he had me sample, or "experience," as he kept saying, about twenty varieties, until I didn't feel like eating any more. Some of the varieties I knew from the grocery store, but others were foreign to me.

"Just one more I want you to try," he said, making his way over to trees that bore larger apples, moving with remarkable agility for an older man with a limp. "You gotta try a Red Delicious. These are common in the supermarket, but there's nothing like one just pulled."

He watched me eat for a second. "Sweet, in a mellow kind of way," he said with satisfaction, smiling as if he had figured me out.

I so didn't want to be one with a softer palette, so, even though my mouth was full, I immediately told him that I preferred the apples with a bit of snap. "It doesn't matter," he chortled, looking at me incredulously. "There's something for everyone here."

We had to walk past the barn to get to the house, and as we approached I realized the barn doors were open to reveal a gaping wound the size of a canyon. There, slumped against the inside wall was the motorcycle. There was a cover slung over it, but the front wheel was so banged up that it wouldn't fit. There was no way to hide the distortion of his life. It was a heartbreaking sight. The gravel under my feet had ceased crunching, which must have triggered him to turn around. I hadn't realized that I had stopped walking. He caught me looking at it before I could think to turn my gaze elsewhere.

"Do you ride?" he asked.

"No," I said, looking into his pained face. "You?"

He had a gentle faraway look that belied his determination. I thought he was resigned to defeat at first. Then something unexpected happened. Something flickered inside him. "Not yet."

☐

The screen door clapped behind me, and I followed Clem down a cool, dark passageway that seemed more like a tunnel at that moment than a country-house hallway. There were doors open on both sides, but it was the glow of soft light and the scent of cinnamon that guided my attention like a lure to the end of the hall. I stretched to see beyond the shadow of Clem's shoulder, eager to learn what I was getting myself into, but his imbalanced gait would permit nothing more than quick pulses of information ... a green wooden chair, the side of a honey-colored hutch, floral wallpaper, a rosebud pattern maybe ... and I resigned myself to saving my neck muscles for a better cause.

"Got one for ya," he called, hanging his coat on a hook in the hall.

"I thought I heard somebody with you," a woman replied. I was amazed that she could hear anything other than the shuffle of Clem's feet. The room was large enough that I had trouble locating the source of the voice. Then there was the flutter of a hand and a smile cast upward that could melt a glacier on a frigid day. She was sitting at one end of a long wooden table, a selection of weathered index cards arranged before her like a quiet game of solitaire. The thread of a tea bag draped over the rim of her mug, and her fingers played on the handle as she spoke to me.

"I was just trying to figure out what to bake. I was beginning to think it would be just me and Nanny Kathleen."

I took a quick look around the room.

"She's not here yet," the woman said, rising to greet me. "I'm Prudence, but you can call me Pru. That's what everybody else does."

"I'm El," I said, sticking with my story.

"How 'bout a cup of tea, El?" Clem called out from the stove as he poured one for himself.

"I don't drink tea, but thank you."

"A nip of scotch?" he asked with a devilish twinkle.

I couldn't hold back a laugh. The offer of hard liquor was so unexpected. "No, thank you. I think we'd all regret it if I started drinking scotch."

"A bit of cider then?"

"Sounds safe enough. Thank you."

Pru motioned me to take a seat across from her. "What would you like to make today, El? I was just mulling it over, trying to come up with something new for me and Nanny to try."

"I really can't say. Whatever you want to make is fine with me," I said. I waited for her to decide, but she waited to hear more from me. "You'll soon see that I don't know my way around a kitchen. It really won't matter one way or another," I added.

"I want you to make something that you can see yourself enjoying at your own table with your family. There's no point in making something you won't eat," she said.

It wasn't a personal question, but it felt like one. The truth embarrassed me. I got the feeling that she wouldn't understand that I rarely ate dessert, and on the rare occasions that I did it was store-bought and I was plopped on a sofa in front of a television set. Mine was a behavior that offered little reverence for her craft. But even more embarrassing was the fact that no one comes to my table.

Her face was soft and hopeful, as if she thought we'd be on common ground if she simply listened long enough. Her strawberry-blonde hair was a perfect complement to her fair complexion, and I wondered whether she colored her hair and if Clem's hair had once been the same color. "I can't promise you that I'd eat anything other than apple pie," I finally said, afraid that I would disappoint her.

"Then an old-fashioned apple pie it will be," she said, beginning to pick up the index cards. I realized only then that they were old recipe cards. The top corners of each card were frayed from fingers walking over them, and the words to the recipes were scribbled in pencil that had long faded. She tenderly filed them away in an old metal box, and a wave of sadness came over me. Apple pie was clearly not a recipe she would need to reference, and I was sorry that I wasn't more inventive for her sake. If she was disappointed, she didn't show it. She moved about the kitchen spryly, collecting bowls and ingredients with ease.

Clem had settled himself in the corner with his tea and a newspaper. I took a sip of the cider he had left for me and began to absorb the surroundings. The room was large and cheerful. Molding separated the walls into upper and lower halves. The top half was a rosebud-patterned wallpaper that looked like it could have been put up in the 70s. The bottom half consisted of vertically placed planks of wood, the color of cream to match the backdrop to the rosebuds. There were a couple of hutches that housed china and a large armoire full of everyday plates, mugs, pots, pans, and bowls. Dispersed between these larger pieces of furniture were upholstered chairs, the kind I was used to seeing in living rooms, only they were now no longer presentable for a formal setting. The legs and armrests were scratched and worn, and the upholstery had a layered effect, as if even the furniture got used to wearing aprons in the kitchen. Clem's chair was matted with towels, undoubtedly to guard it from the inevitable filth he brought in with him.

"Nanny, I thought you'd never get here!" Pru yelled toward the door. I jumped in my seat, but no one seemed to notice. For a second I thought Pru had lost a few marbles, that she was speaking to a vision only she could see, but then I could hear a faint pitter-patter coming down the hall, accompanied by heavy breathing that became more audible with every step.

"I had to go halfway back. I forgot your blueberries," Nanny mustered, puffing her way into the room.

"Quick change in plans," Pru said, leaning into me, seven or eight apples cradled in her arms. "Can you manage an apple-blueberry pie instead?" she whispered, her eyes pleading. "I plum forgot Nanny was bringing the blueberries. She'd be so disappointed if we didn't use them."

"Not a problem at all," I said, trying to sound reassuring. I was actually relieved to be adding another ingredient to the mix. She flashed a quick grateful smile, her eyes bright and wide, her brows arched, as if to say, "You know how Nanny can be." I turned to look at Nanny, who was finally approaching the table.

"Well who do we have here?" Nanny crooned, focusing through thick, finger-smudged bifocals. Her salt-and-pepper hair had a frizzy texture that I imagined was hard to tame. It was swept up in a loose bun, from which plenty of crimped strands had escaped. Her shoulder bones emerged from her housecoat like two pop tents, and I thought if I exhaled too hard I would blow her over. She peered through her lenses as if she were examining the contents of a petri dish and she needed to determine whether I was bacteria of a volatile nature. "Well she's lovely," she determined. I couldn't quite put my finger on it, but there was something a bit off about Nanny, although her heart seemed to be in the right place.

We baked the better part of the afternoon away, Pru and Nanny showing me how to peel, core, and slice the apples to a good size. Then we stirred the slices in large bowls until each one wore a thick coat of sugar and cinnamon. Nanny would intermittently ask us to stop stirring so that she could toss in more blueberries. Once we had made a half dozen apple-blueberry pies, Nanny was interested in moving on to the next blueberry recipe. She started to prepare the dough while I sauntered around the kitchen with my cider in hand, intoxicated by the sweet aroma, ready to die a happy death.

Their chatter about the locals played like soft music in the backdrop of my thoughts. The fine china in the hutches looked as though it could have been a hundred years old. Many of the pieces had been glued back together. I liked that. To me, it was a reflection of the family's resilience. If Nanny wanted to use blueberries, so be it. We'll work with her on that. If we break a one-hundred-year-old plate, so what? We'll just glue it back together again, they would say to each other. I liked thinking that this was a family that picked up the pieces, a family that made the best of what was left behind.

A loud bang was followed by quick, heavy footsteps, and I found myself taking several steps back to the security of the table. Clem looked up from his paper, his eyes elevating from behind his reading glasses. "That would be Finn" he said, adding "my son," as if there was nothing to say about the racket, as if he had adequately explained in that one sentence that the stampede of The Light Brigade was an everyday occurrence.

Finn crossed the room like a determined tornado. He carried a crate full of quivering bottles to a refrigerator on the far wall. There were no greetings, no glances. "Finn, I want you to meet El," Clem called out from the corner. Only then did Finn offer a quick look that revealed nothing about him.

Although I knew he was sired by the old man, he was a horse of a different color. There was nothing outwardly gentle about him. In fact, his nature was somewhat fiery, like that of a long-hungry bull. His field of vision seemed intentionally narrow too. He had a job to do, and he chose to concentrate on it. If he hadn't been pulled from it, an enormous irritation to him, I'm quite sure he never would have noticed me at all. I had traveled halfway across the kitchen to introduce myself, and I stood there what seemed an eternity, my powder-puff hand reaching out to a vast abyss. Only after an embarrassing length of time did I allow my hand to meet my thigh once again, and in a motion that would have registered rejection to anyone paying attention, I absently wiped the excess flour into the corduroy ridges of my skirt, forming my own emblazoned declaration of shame and defeat.

"The girl was holding her hand out to you, Finn," Clem called. No reply came. Finn just kept unloading the bottles from the crate and placing them in the refrigerator. I didn't know whether he heard Clem or not, but I was guessing he did.

Before I recovered enough to cower into a corner, Nanny made her way to me, taking my hands in hers, stretching our arms to form a bridge wide enough for any overgrown child interested in playing games. I wanted to ask what she was doing, but my mouth wouldn't move.

"Finn, take a look at her," she said, beginning to spin me around the room. "Isn't she marvelous? ... Isn't she beautiful?" I gripped her hands firmly in an effort to break the momentum, but the unanticipated sensation of squeezing clumped blue veins against fragile bones was more nauseating than the rotation. I finally managed to slow her to a halt, but she was still enamored. "She's gorgeous," she said.

Finn clanked the last bottle down hard in the refrigerator and elevated out of his working squat. With his hands on his hips he began to circle us, his eyes glaring at me. "She is," he said, in a mocking tone. "She's beautiful."

"Yes," Nanny agreed, oblivious to the sarcasm.

"She's like a beautiful clown," Finn said, his voice lilting like Nanny's, oozing false affection.

"She is," Nanny said.

"She's like a beautiful, clumsy clown," Finn sang. Whereas *clown* had been perfectly acceptable to her, thankfully *clumsy* triggered disapproval.

"Well, I don't know about clumsy," she snapped, releasing my hands as if a wand had just released her from her spell. "She's not clumsy," she said, making her way back to her position at the table.

I probably should have made my way back too, but my feet wouldn't go anywhere, my gaze wouldn't leave him. It was my last chance at any kind of dignity. He would have to look away first. I knew he probably didn't see it that way, like a game. He was probably unaware that I was fighting tooth and nail for something. And sure enough he just kept looking at me, his hands on his hips, his eyes piercing through me like steely blue daggers. His face was getting ruddy too, which only intensified the blue in his eyes. The physical commentary relayed a message that never came verbally but was crystal clear nonetheless: What the hell are *you* looking at?

I held my ground for a long time, but awkwardness began to set in. He changed his stance, folding his arms over his chest and tilting his head to the side, as if expressing curiosity, but the kind of curiosity one would have in an oddity. I could feel the fingers in my right hand beginning to tingle. *Oh God, Ellen, don't do it. Don't try to introduce yourself again.* But before I could he flared his nostrils, and all I could think was that he was like a kettle that had finally boiled. His eyelids lowered halfway, as if to say I was a joke, and there was a quick grunt too. Then he grabbed the empty crate in one stealthy, swooping motion and left as suddenly as he came. The showdown was over, and I had won. So why were my thighs emitting a heat I had never felt before, making me feel like I had lost? Why did it feel like he left with more than an empty crate?

I turned to discover I had a captivated audience of only two. Nanny was kneading a ball of dough, ignorant to what she had initiated, but the elder brother and sister stood with their mouths agape. I hadn't noticed any sibling similarity until that moment, but it was clear that they shared the same look of shock. I waited for them to say something, anything, and when neither one did, I spoke. "I suppose I should be on my way."

"Don't go," Pru said, pressing her hands into her apron as she turned to Clem. There was a long pause as Clem stood there scratching the side of his head.

"I don't know what to say," he started. "Finn," he said, pointing toward the door, "is ... difficult ... stubborn. Sometimes it's just plain uncomfortable to be around him ... and that's not easy to say about your own son. Anyway, he's not likely to come back for a while ... if you want to finish making your pie." He looked to Pru, then back at me. "I wish you'd stay ... please finish."

"I really can't. I'm sorry," I said, collecting my things, glancing at my watch for effect. "It's not Finn. Believe me, it has nothing to do with him. It's just getting late, and I really have to get going." And it really wasn't Finn. It was more my reaction to him that I had to process, alone. I had never met anyone that intense, that honest before. It was enormously refreshing actually. He was so unforgivably rude, but it felt strangely good to be thrown for a loop.

Clem walked me out. "I'm really sorry for your uneasiness. I wish I could make it up to you," he said with earnest.

"You really have nothing to apologize for, really. I had a wonderful day, and I thank you for that."

"I could help you with your book," he offered, the words taking a desperate tumble out of his mouth. I turned around to face him, and there was the silence of a cold, windless evening setting in. "If that's what you want to do, I mean, write a book about apple farming, then I could help you with that." I could see his breath as he spoke, and his face was almost pleading with me. There was something so good about him. So decent. He wasn't the kind of man to forget a dream. I wished it were my dream. How many people find someone so knowledgeable, so well-intentioned, to help them with a dream? I willed it to be my dream.

"Okay," I said.

"Then you'll come soon again?"

"Yes." I could see my breath too. "I'll come soon again." We shook hands, a pact that was a mixture of determination and relief, and I watched him go back inside, the screen door thumping behind him like a soft kiss. The screen door to this house, I mused, was a true predictor of one's mood and personality. And unlike me, it never lied.

I became one with the darkness as I crunched my way down the graveled drive. I turned back around to see the house silhouetted by a sun that had almost set. The sky had cleared, and the stars were making themselves known. A light went on in the front room, but I couldn't see anyone inside.

I didn't find any answers. If anything I left with more questions. And wonder, particularly about the polarity of Clem and Finn. Those two pulled me in so many different directions ... I felt like my heart was going to jump right out of my chest. But for the first time in a long time, I felt alive. My heart was pounding, but I was breathing easily. Pure, natural, sweet adrenaline. And as I left them, I could think of little else but returning. Oh Johnnie ... what a ride.

Chapter 7

Revelations, Not

"Oh no. No ... no ... no ... no," Jules moaned as she repeatedly thumped her head against her desk.

"What on earth is the matter with you?" I asked.

"It's worse than I ever thought. Oh my God, you're in worse shape than I ever dreamed."

"What are you talking about?"

"Oh my God," she gasped.

"Jules, get a hold of yourself. What's the matter?"

"You've fallen for a 78-year-old apple farmer. I knew I should have gone with you."

At this I quickly grabbed her forearm and scanned the reception area for another breathing soul. Thankfully I couldn't find one to repeat what she had said. "Jules, are you insane? Where are you getting this from? Nothing could be further from the truth. I have no idea what you're talking about. And for God's sake, keep your voice down."

She looked at me deeply, and I held her gaze good and firm. I memorized the position and shape of every black speck that decorated those hazel irises while Tom Petty's "I Won't Back

Down" began to strum in my head. "False," I mouthed, knowing that she heard it but hoping that peripherally she could also make out the shape of the word.

"Okay," she said, bluffing for a second, not ready to look away just yet. "Okay," she said again, still looking for any possible sign of waiver. "Okay," she said, now beginning to nod, now breathing again. "But something's up," she said, raising her finger to me. "I know you, Ellen Bannister, and you're not this happy." And she was entirely serious.

The elevator dinged and voices began to spill into the waiting area as the doors parted. "We'll talk later," I said, moving away from her, locking eyes with her long enough to indicate that I meant business.

I slid behind my desk, still in my coat, and began to loosen the scarf from my neck, feeling as though I had saved myself from the gallows. I sat there for a second in disbelief, saying "What the?" out loud. Julie wasn't usually that far off base, but this one was right out of left field. Good God, how could she think I'd be that desperate?

I slid the drawer open and pulled out the two letters for a quick review. Now that I had met Clem I wondered how much of him I would see in the letters. Like Clem himself, the paper was good stock. I had probably read the letters a dozen or more times since I had received them. A cheaper paper would have started to tear at the creases. Just two letters, yet they spoke volumes about him. He was vulnerable, yet determined. He was as sad as he was content. He was a fixer, frustrated with something that couldn't be fixed. Above all, I saw him as a healer who needed to be healed himself. Heck, didn't we all need a little healing?

And what about the son? What was going on there? Why did he blame himself for his sister's death? That was something I couldn't relate to. I think I would have curled up and died if I felt guilt about John's death. If guilt had been part of the equation, where would I be now? You obviously never get over a loss that deep. It's a process. My theory on it was that it was okay to get stuck once in a while, but you had to keep moving through it. Not "moving on." I hated that expression. But moving through it. I knew all about problems that couldn't be fixed. The rest of our lives would be about moving through it.

Finn was a lot to take on in my head, but I kept thinking about him. I was fascinated by his anger. I knew it must serve some purpose, but I couldn't wrap my head around how it was productive. In many ways he was my parallel. I didn't know any adults my age who suddenly lost an only sibling. Then we went perpendicular on the anger issue. I never had that anger. In my heart and soul I respected it though. I couldn't relate to it, but I respected it.

I was more relaxed when I thought about Clem. It was easier to concentrate on him and to try to figure out a way to gently pull information from him, something that would give me some indication of how we were connected. Asking him flat out was not an option. I knew this more now than ever. He was just so sweet, so gentle, so giving. He was an old man. He didn't deserve to be embarrassed about his feelings, which he would undoubtedly be if I told him who I was. I wasn't sure if I was ready for the truth anyway. It would take a little time to get to the bottom of it all, but that was okay. Although Clem was 78, I got the feeling he had some good days left in him. All thoughts of Clem eventually wove back to Finn. I got the feeling that Finn had answers for me too, and I got the feeling he was the one more in danger of dying.

Why did I feel so compelled to see both of them again? Sure I was curious about why he was writing to me. It was like a mystery I had to solve. But it was more than that too. It always came back to John. It always came back to figuring out how to hold his essence close to me. He embraced life. I had to be more like him. How do I do that? Not him exactly, but I wanted to take his best qualities and make them my own. It was a way to honor him, a way to make him part of my world forever, a way toward something deeper and richer, and a way to ask more of myself than I ever did before. In theory, it was a good way to mourn him. Putting it all into practice, though, was another story.

So how would he go about doing this? He always seemed to reintroduce himself with such ease. He would meet someone once and have no trouble greeting them the second time. I always worried that I wouldn't be remembered. And the truth is I often wasn't. I had mentioned this to John one night at Triumph after he introduced me to someone he had only met once before.

"Who cares whether they remember you or not?" he asked.

"I do," I said. "I care."

"The trick is not to take it so personally, El. You think everyone always remembers me? They don't. The point is you remember them, so say hello." He thought about what he was trying to convey, and then shrugged his shoulders. "Make them feel special, even if you got a bad feel from them the first time. People are fragile. And sometimes it's just shyness. They need reassurance sometimes, to be the best they can be, to be who they really are."

"You are what they call an idealist," I told him, but it fell on deaf ears.

"When you meet someone for the second time, it can almost be categorized," he continued. "Sometimes you make eye contact and you look away for a second, but you both know you saw each other. And often enough you both have some recollection of who the other is. What takes place after that makes all the difference in the world. Never walk away because it's a little awkward. It leaves you empty. I'd rather see you go for it. I'd rather you put yourself out there. There are those who put themselves out there, maybe struggle a bit for the name, but they make an honest effort. They meet you halfway. I admire these people, the ones who want to reach beyond the awkwardness. They make sure you know they remembered you. Then there are those who pretend they didn't see you, because it's just easier for them that way. Then there are those who walk in a shroud of aloofness, I swear just hoping that you will approach them so that they can pretend they don't remember you."

"Yeah, like you know what that's like," I said, feeling my eyes roll to the back of my head.

"Then every once in a while, El, you meet someone and they change your life for the better," he said, surveying the vicinity for some on-hand examples. The bastard had a room full of them. "You put yourself out there enough, El, every once in a while you get lucky. You meet … genuineness," he said, with an all-knowing smile on his face, happy with his word choice. "You meet someone and they can't wait to tell you that they remember your name and that they're glad to see you again. And when it happens, it's a gift. It's a good feeling that stays with you for a while."

It was late in the night, and at that point he probably had one more than he should have, but he still made a lot of sense. John never really appeared drunk, and I'm not sure he ever was. "Where does he put it?" people would ask. His tie was in a loose loop around his neck, and the top button of his shirt was undone.

His jacket hung loosely on a body that was spent until he had a good night's rest. He was a bit overdue for a haircut, and the natural waviness was growing in. At one point Katherine came over and gave the mop a good shake. "Ellen, don't listen to him. Not at this hour," she said, holding a glass of red wine in one hand, turning her wrist to check her watch. She looked out for him. They often mingled in different groups, but she always came back to him, playfully touching him. Even now, four years later, I can still hear her melodic laughter in my head, joy that never should have been silenced. And he adored her. He would grab her arm and stroke it while he continued to speak to me, as if to say to her, *Don't go anywhere,* without ever speaking a word. A highly social creature, she would move on, but she would return periodically for closeness.

"There are all kinds of people in this world," he continued. I couldn't help but notice his eyes fall on Brian, who was sitting by himself at an empty table playing his new Gameboy. He had his black canvas sneakers propped up on a chair, one ankle over the other. He was an undignified sight in his orange and brown striped T-shirt, his army-green knapsack, right out of the seventies, thrown carelessly across the table. "And there's room for most of them too," John said, stifling laughter. I couldn't hold mine in. I knew John liked Brian, but they had so little in common. Brian was my husband, and even I had little in common with him. John and Katherine, on the other hand, were social beings, and I wanted to absorb whatever social graces I could from them, hoping that the combination of dim lighting, alcohol, laughter, and something unseen in the air between 3 and 4 a.m. would magically bring about the process of osmosis. My skin would become as permeable as that of a cell membrane, and then I too could soak up their enthusiasm, laugh freely and be as light as air.

But looking at Brian, I knew that there were people who needed nothing more than a 3 x 3 screen to find happiness. I didn't pity Brian, nor did John. Quite to the contrary, there was much to envy. He never seemed to want anything he couldn't have.

"You're sensitive, El," John said, leaning back on his stool to take me in, to offer his analysis. "It's one of your best qualities," he said, smiling, but painfully serious now. "It is arguably *the* best thing about you. It's what I admire most in you. You sense when someone else is hurting because you've been hurt so many times yourself. You wear your heart on your sleeve. Ironically, the best thing about you is what embarrasses you the most. You hate that you're so soft. It's a wonderful quality, El. Anyone can be outgoing. All you have to do is put your mind to it really. But not everyone sees into others the way that you do. That's a gift."

"Well I have to argue with you there, buddy," I said. "It's not just a decision you make to be outgoing. If that were the case everyone would be a magnet for fun. What you have is charisma, and not everyone has that."

It was becoming a ridiculous conversation, a sibling love fest, each of us patting the other on the back. You spend your whole adolescent life bickering, and if you're lucky enough you reach adulthood together and you're still talking. And if you're really lucky, you appreciate each other. You see each other in a whole new light. John and I lost our parents to a car accident when we were young, and the only real consistency we had in life was each other. He was my past and my present, the longest relationship of my life, a parent and sibling rolled into one. And the future? I thought he was my future too, but when the future arrives it's the present, and my present doesn't have John in it anymore.

I remembered saying to him, "You know we wouldn't be having this conversation at a normal hour. One isn't inclined to get this sappy at three o'clock in the afternoon."

"All I'm saying is you get what you give," he continued, taking another sip from a half-drained bottle of Coors Light. "You get what you put out there. It really is that simple. You have to put yourself out there, and see what comes back to you. And you do have charisma, missy," he said, laughing, pointing his finger at me. I loved it when he called me missy. It had made me feel like I had just talked back to him and that I actually had some sass in me. It had made me laugh.

I liked Clem and Finn. They were genuine people. I liked that they consumed my thoughts. So many of my thoughts over the last four years were about John, and while I always felt he was with me, watching me, it got lonely from time to time. I would wake to his voice in my head: *You gotta start hanging out with some living people, El. You're going to be there a while. Get comfortable.* Well here they were. These were real, living people—ones I could relate to—and I got the feeling they really cared about each other, which made me care about them.

Chapter 8

Another Visit

It wasn't supposed to be this hard. The second visit was supposed to be infinitely easier than the first. I just sat there looking up the long graveled drive, thinking Mount Everest couldn't look more ominous. I reminded myself that there was room at the top for the car. I didn't have to leave it at the bottom like I did the week before. It wasn't that bold a move to drive up this time. There was room for the car, and there was room for me. *If you're going to enter their world, enter it fully and unapologetically right from the get-go,* I told myself.

I put the car in Drive and asked myself for courage. I put the car in Park and stalled emotionally, my heart racing. I wasn't one to sweat a lot, but I swear I could feel moisture on my brow. *He said it was okay if you came back. You looked forward to it all week, you dumb ass.* I eventually realized that this sort of negativity wasn't helping. I loosened my grip on the wheel.

I put the car in Drive one more time, dipping into the fuel reserves of my past, knowing that they were high-grade enough to get me through my future. That's how I see relationships now. Those with substance will offer you power when you're on your own. I listened to the wheels fight hard for friction, spitting the gravel out behind them, nice and gritty. Surprise entrances weren't possible here.

Once I reached the top Clem was visible immediately, walking toward me from the barn, wiping his hands in an already filthy towel that was half submerged in the well of his rear pocket. He was squinting, trying to make out who I was. I was instantly sorry I came. Anything short of immediate recognition heightened my insecurity. While a big deal to me, my visit of a week earlier was probably long forgotten. I had a sick feeling that he would look long and hard into my face and end up with nothing more to say than, "Can I help you?" I couldn't bear to look at him approaching any longer. It was easier to focus on the *H* at the center of the steering wheel, symbolizing this week's rental, a Honda. Then, penetrating through glass, I could hear him, his voice like a welcoming trumpet: "El, is that you?"

Before I lifted my eyes from the wheel, I remember saying to myself, *Genuineness ... pure genuineness. Jackpot, I just hit the mother lode of genuineness.* I opened the car door and there was nothing between us again. The second greeting was over, and it was beginning to feel like there would never be barriers between us. I couldn't possibly put into words the trust I felt I could place in him at that moment.

"I didn't know you'd come so soon again, but I'm glad you did. To be perfectly blunt, I didn't know if you'd come at all." He patted me on the shoulder and squeezed my hand. "But I'm glad you did." He flashed a warm smile, and then with a quick wave of his hand he directed me toward the house, saying "Well come on. You have to come say hello to Pru and Nanny. They're in there, just as you left them."

But they weren't entirely as I had left them. The focus had changed from baking to knitting. Pru came over for a hug when she realized it was me. It made me uncomfortable, I guess because it was unexpected. I wondered if she felt sorry for me. I was angry with myself for not knowing how to respond. What effort would it have taken me to lift my arms up for a halfhearted embrace? There wasn't much time to dwell on it, though. Clem was moving quickly through the kitchen. "I just want to get myself a cup of tea. And then we need to talk," he said, looking back at me. "Cider, wasn't it?"

It startled me that he remembered what I had to drink last time. I normally didn't drink tea, but it was damp and I asked for a cup. Maybe I was searching for camaraderie, for some uniting force, or maybe just for common ground. He didn't question it. He washed his hands, filled two mugs with boiling water, palmed a couple of tea bags, and led the way. "Where are you going without the cream and sugar, Clem?" Pru called after him.

"It's okay," he said, shaking her off with a brisk nod of his head. "She doesn't drink tea anyway, so she won't know the difference." *God damn, if the bugger didn't remember every detail about me.*

I wasn't sure what the destination was, but it was good to see some of what lay beyond the swinging door of the kitchen. As we left, I could hear Pru explaining to Nanny that I was the girl they had baked with the week before, and Nanny responding, "Who? Who is she?"

He led me through a foyer that was homey, yet surprisingly formal. I had wrongly assumed that the rest of the house would be as lived-in as the kitchen. Gold-and-cream striped wallpaper played a backdrop to dark oil paintings in gilded frames. The bumpy, wooden-planked floors, embedded with age-old pine knots, had to be original to the house. They were hearty and well cared for, with a shine that indicated a recent polish. A door left ajar revealed a large blue formal dining room, with cushion-backed chairs and Dutch blue and white porcelain sconces on the walls. I couldn't imagine why this room was necessary. Clem and Pru didn't seem the type to do a lot of entertaining. On the other side of the foyer was a large sitting room. He led me out to the front porch, where we settled in a couple of cushioned wicker chairs overlooking the front of the property. It seemed he was comfortable here, and he allowed the weight of his body to sink into the cushions fully before he spoke.

"I've been thinking about your book," he said. "I can help you if it's regional. I know about farming apples in this region like I know about the back of my hand." At this, he examined his hand, with all its creases and age spots. He then took a long sip from his tea, the heat of it wrapping around his face like a warm blanket. He gulped hard and continued. "I can't pretend to know about growing apples in California, or even an hour north of here for that matter. But I'll give ya everything I got if we're talking this land right here, if we're talking Cider Banks or the nearby area."

I didn't say anything to this. I didn't know he was waiting for me to respond.

"Are you still game?" he asked, after a few seconds of silence.

"Still game for what?" I asked.

"To write a book," he said.

"Oh, yes," I leapt in, feeling bad that I hadn't made this clear by nodding or showing some other form of enthusiasm.

"I don't know what timeframe you had in mind, but we could do this several different ways," he continued. "We could do it month by month, where I would show you what we do here on a monthly basis. You may be the type that needs to observe firsthand before you can record information, before you can put it all into words that make sense to most. Only drawback is that you'd need a whole year, and I don't know if you have that kind of time on your hands. Or you may be the type who studies books. Perhaps you're more of a researcher, in which case I suspect you won't need me so much. You could read about what we do year-round in books. You don't need me so much for that."

There was another lull in the conversation. He was waiting to hear from me. "I don't know how you learn," he said. "You're going to have to tell me how you learn."

It was so remarkably simple, but few would think to ask. He made enormous sense. His approach required that I know myself, which, for me, was the scary part. Somehow he must have sensed I struggled with this. Maybe he sensed that I just wanted to spend time with him. I'm not sure which.

"It's okay," he said. "We can figure that out."

The sound of tires laboring up the drive caught his attention, and he turned to see who it was. "Finn's back," he said, stretching to see him, but not long enough for me to figure out who I was.

He turned back around. "It's okay, ya know," never forgetting where he left off. "We can figure that out. We can see what works best for you."

Another vehicle spun up the drive, a woman this time. There was no sun that day, but her hoop earrings were large enough to reflect some light. Her hair was dark and long. I could see this much. Clem watched her come up the drive, his face expressionless.

"Is that his girlfriend?" I asked.

"Girlfriend?" he snorted in disbelief, suppressing laughter. He leaned in as if he had a secret to share. "Let me put it to you this way. Finn has *girls,* and there isn't one among them he can consider *a friend."*

Clem got up and walked to the edge of the porch. I followed him. The two of us watched her get out of the car and storm Finn. Her jeans were tight, too tight, painted on. In spite of this constriction, she threw her hands into Finn's chest with enough force to make him fall back a few strides. Finn seemed unfazed by her aggression, as if this type of display were common to him. I looked at Clem, and he too seemed unfazed. He didn't even search for an outcome. He didn't see a need to intervene. He didn't seem to care.

"Why don't we start in the orchard? Clarity can always be found in the orchard," he said. He began walking downhill, and I followed him, not sure whether he could truly put what he had seen behind him. But somewhere in the neat, organized rows and spidery branches I realized that he could find a temporary shelter from any storm. An elevating calm came over him with each stride, and he began to talk about his land. He had 250 acres— what he considered a small farm—and as he spoke I couldn't help but think of him as a shepherd with a flock. He knew and cared for every tree, spoke about the different varieties as if they were people with personalities. With the exception of fifteen peach trees, he grew nothing but apple trees, his clear preference.

"The peach trees will only last about fifteen years, and then they're done. They're not going to produce any more fruit after that. But an apple tree … Well there's stamina in an apple tree. An apple tree will live a hundred years," he said, with a reserved pride, as if this was a fact that should be quietly marveled, as all wonderful and inexplicable things should be. He pointed to trees that were planted by his father, some in or around the year of his birth.

As I listened to him talk, words from his letter came back to me: *I am a bit of a slow bloomer, of which I am strangely proud.* The life of an apple tree seemed to be seamlessly woven into his own. Time and the stamina to work through it were appealing forces in his world. I could think of no occupation in life that so directly reflected one's self as Clem's. He was what he did. It was impossible to think of him doing anything else. As far as professions go, he had reached a level of satisfaction most can only dream about.

"Trees need time and, like many people, they need space." I didn't want to read too much into that one, but I had a pretty good idea that he knew at least one person who needed more than the average person's share of space. "You want to plant apple trees so that they are forty feet apart from each other on all sides. This will give the roots room to stretch, and it will maximize sunlight interception. You don't want the branch of one tree on top of another, which leads me to the first lesson. It's fall, and we prune in the fall. I don't want to get too technical on you your first time out, but pruning should be seen as nothing less than a combination of art, science, and history. It deserves that much respect, because the cuts you make this season will affect you for two to three years to come."

"Can you ever cut too much?" I asked.

"Yes," he said, lowering and raising his head in one swift swoop. He began looking at me earnestly, his eyes begging me to appreciate how serious a matter it was. "It's a very delicate balance. You cut too much or in the wrong places, it's like saying something biting that you could regret for years. You love your trees, you want to nurture them. You want to maximize their sunlight exposure without compromising their vital organs, so to speak. I'll show you what I mean," he said, working his way to the center of one of his smaller trees. "You see this branch here? This is what we call a central leader. You never prune your central leader. You need the central leader to nourish the offshoot branches. Sometimes the offshoot branches get a little too big for their breeches, so to speak, and you have to remove the two or three largest limbs in the top half of the tree.

"See this one here?" he asked, clasping a thick branch on the top half of the tree. "This is more than half the size of the central leader. A branch of this size will choke the central leader. Your tree will never reach optimal fruiting capacity if your central leader is choked. You know what I'm saying?" he asked, straining his neck back to see that I understood.

"Yep," I said, "I get it. I totally get it." And I did get it. I had my pen and paper out, and I was taking notes. I understood the lesson, but I also kept thinking that he was talking about more than the pruning of an apple tree. He had this way about him that made everything seem like a life lesson, and I couldn't help but think that he saw himself as the central leader and that he was in danger of being choked by an offspring. I thought about asking him if he ever felt like a central leader, but then I had this vision of him looking puzzled by the question, saying, "Heh? What's that you're asking me?" And then I'd have to clarify and say, "You know … do you ever feel like you're the central leader and you're being choked by an offspring?" And then he would wave me off in disgust, saying, "Ahhh, you're just a silly girl from the city!" And then he'd never want to see me again. So I didn't ask, even though I thought it was a pretty good question for him.

"The point is," he said, emerging from the center suddenly, causing me to backstep out of the tree, "all of this is for the overall benefit of the tree, so don't feel bad about snipping here and there. But like I said, two or three of the larger limbs on top is all you want to take."

Then he raised his finger in the air. "Hey, you know what might be neat?" He wasn't looking at me when he said this, so I wasn't sure if he was waiting for an answer.

"What?" I asked eventually, but he didn't answer. He had already made up his mind.

"Yeah. Come on with me." And he began to walk up to the house with purpose. When we reached the top he pointed to a beat-up pickup. "Climb on in to the passenger seat. The door's open. I just want to get my keys." He came out sporting his soiled jacket, waving his keys in the air as he approached. Funny how he didn't need the jacket in the privacy of his own land, but it was necessary to wear it out in public.

"Where are we going?" I asked, as he revved a motor that defied the outward appearance of the vehicle. It was an old truck, with a hood like a bubble and powder-blue paint giving way to rust in places. The door creaked as I shut it. It was loveable. There was nothing edgy about it.

"I want to show you something," he said, offering nothing more. We drove in silence for awhile, and I welcomed the opportunity to be a passenger as well as the anticipation of not knowing where we were going. I knew I'd be safe with him. While I can't say the old pickup was comfortable, I was able to close my eyes and let the intermittent shade of Cider Banks' one-hundred-year-old trees dance like shadow puppets across my face.

Five minutes into the drive he told me where we were going. "The Cider Banks Historical Society is holding a picture exhibit of the last one hundred years of apple farming in Cider Banks."

The thought of going to a photography exhibit was appealing, and I wrongly assumed that the building that housed the The

Cider Banks Historical Society would be as charming as the exhibit itself sounded. Moments later we pulled into the parking lot of a municipal building. I forgot to expect that there would be buildings like this everywhere, even in Cider Banks. Clem escorted me in the back door, where I approached an elevator just feet away. "Oh no, that thing takes too long," he said, gesturing for me to follow as he began hobbling down a flight of stairs, the fluorescent light casting a silver hue at the split. A linoleum floor paved the way through a hall of high-gloss cream paint. The doors lining the hall were tan, my least favorite color in the Crayola box. The hall ended with double swing doors, above which someone had discovered an opportunity to practice their calligraphy. The words *Senior Center*, painted in dark brown, fell left of center, the last two letters of greater width than the others.

Clem pushed through the doors as if he owned the place, calling out, "Hank, where are ya?" I began to follow him, as I always did, but he waved me off. "Just wait here a second, El." He walked through a large paneled room and disappeared into a well-lit room that I could only imagine was a kitchen. Fold-up tables and chairs were leaned against the paneling like long-forgotten wallflowers. He emerged a minute later with a set of keys, and I followed him back into the hall, where he fumbled with the keys outside one of the doors to the left. While he struggled to find the one that fit the lock, I noticed a more sophisticated attempt at calligraphy on the door. This time the brown letters, forming the words *Cider Banks Historical Society*, were traced in a paint of golden glitter and were perfectly centered. He swung the door open and flipped on the lights, revealing a pleasant reading room that had the feel of a library, with plain wooden tables and chairs and brand-new wall-to-wall industrial carpeting. The lighting

81

was soft, and the walls were lined with photographs, all of them covered in frames of Plexiglas.

We started with the ones to the left of the door, since Clem indicated that the photographs were arranged in chronological order. He knew a little something about everyone in the pictures, even the ones that dated back almost a hundred years, and I soon found myself transported by his stories. Terry Brennan ran a distillery out of his cellar during Prohibition—"best spiked cider around"—and Banjo Burke played banjo at his midnight parties. He explained that most of these people he never knew and that most of the older stories were hearsay, tales passed down through the generations, but I could tell he treasured them nonetheless. As we worked our way around the room, it became clear to me that there was a rich social history here, good backdrop information for our book, I thought.

When we came to his own time period he began to point out uncles and cousins, many of them deceased and many of them just plain gone, as well as their farms. Many of the photos had a snapshot quality to them, with frayed borders and creases marbled through them, and others were in excellent condition. Many were surprisingly intimate, close-ups of faces beaded with sweat, clothes soiled with earth, mothers holding the tiny hands of toddlers.

There was one of a woman having a talk with a young boy while the tear-streaked face of a little girl looked on. The woman cradled the boy's cheeks in her palms so that he was forced to look at her. He had one leg stretched out behind him, ready to bolt as soon as he was released. Even though the photograph didn't appear to be that old, the white borders had already browned in an honest sepia. I say honest because in publishing we were always asking book designers to add a sepia tint to give the effect of age.

It was like cheating. We might have a crisp black-and-white print of an old-fashioned telephone, the kind where the funnel-shaped receiver dangles from a hook on the side. Of course readers would know it's an old phone by looking at it, but because of the new print, it wouldn't *feel* like an old phone. It wouldn't necessarily evoke the passage of time. So we'd ask a designer to put a sepia tint on it. And voilà! Suddenly it *felt* like we were looking at an original print, which somehow made us feel like we were back in the 1800s. It was a trick, yes, but it was fair. We all like to feel like we're going back in time once in awhile, maybe Clem and I more than most. Heck, Clem and I probably wished we could bathe in sepia every day, sink right in like we were slipping into a bubble bath. I was captivated by this one photograph. He usually spoke before I had much time to use my imagination, but he had turned quiet on me.

"What about them?" I asked, turning to him. "Do you know them?"

"I do," he said, in deep thought. "I took that picture on Halloween, about thirty-five years ago. That's my wife with Finn, and the little girl is my daughter, Judith." My stomach instantly dropped out of me. There was no way to see this conversation coming, and I wasn't prepared for it. Clem started to laugh softly. "My wife was giving Finn a gentle lecture on how the other children were also entitled a turn at apple bobbing."

There were details that I had to remember not to remember, things I knew from the letters that I couldn't mention. I would bet money that he remembered everything that he told me in person. He was remarkable that way. *Just keep it simple,* I thought, *Just keep it honest.* "She was beautiful," I said.

"She was. She died twenty-one years ago. Breast cancer."

Before I could think of anything else to say, he started to chuckle. "Poor Finn, he couldn't wait to get his head back in that barrel. He always had more energy than he knew what to do with. Try as we would, we couldn't temper it. Until he took up carpentry, he never really had a place to funnel it. And even that only helps to a degree."

He grew silent again, and I thought about what I would say next if I had never gotten a letter, if I didn't know anything about him. I knew I would ask about Judith, for a couple of reasons. I would want to know where she was, yes. But beyond a mere curiosity, I would want him to know that I cared where she was. I would want him to know that I cared about his life.

"What about Judith?" I asked. "Where is she now?" And just like that, I had asked him to go back in time, to revisit something unpleasant. Although I knew I had to start asking him questions like this, I still felt as if I had washed our relationship in sepia, a dishonest one.

He took a deep breath, and told me in a matter-of-fact way, not looking for sympathy, just revealing the facts. "Judith died in a motorcycle accident four years ago. She was up from New York for a long weekend. As was her habit, she was just going into town to get a coffee and a paper, just saying hi and hello to some of the locals. It was early and misty." Then he turned to me, shrugging, "Tire must have lost traction."

"I'm sorry ... about Judith and your wife."

"I know," he said. And after that he said nothing for awhile. There isn't much you can say in response to *I'm sorry*. I know that. I usually say *Thank you*, but sometimes it sounds trite. I may have felt uncomfortable if I didn't know what it was like to be on the receiving end of *I'm sorry*, but because I knew, I didn't mind the silence. There was something more honest about the silence. We drove back in silence too. He asked if I wanted to come in, but I felt I needed a little space. Maybe we both needed a little space.

Before I got out of the truck he said, "You know, El, you can always stay with us while you do your research. We have plenty of room. We used to run an inn a few years back. There are plenty of beds upstairs with crisp sheets on them, just waiting for somebody to occupy them again." He waited for me to consider the offer. I didn't say anything at first, even though I thought it would be nice to stay in their big old house and sip tea with him in the evenings. "Just something to keep in mind. Might be easier for you," he added.

I slid off the passenger seat, and turned to look back up at him. "I might take you up on that."

"I wish you would. Plenty of room. We'd love to have you. It'd be good for us to have an overnight visitor again."

It was hard to say goodbye to him, both of us so melancholy. At least I knew I was, and I had a feeling he might be. I reached back in to squeeze his arm, just like he had squeezed my hand at the beginning of the day. "Thank you for today."

"You got it," he said, with a swift swoop of his head. He did that often, a motion that conveyed his own endearing mixture of sincerity and persuasion, as if he couldn't wait to let me know he meant what he said. He no longer needed to persuade me of his sincerity. I knew in my heart and soul that he was true blue.

□

I didn't feel like driving home just yet. There were days when I couldn't wait to get home, to let the small confines of my studio apartment shelter me. Then there were days when it felt like the four walls were suffocating me, compressing my sadness further into me. I thought it would be one of the latter. Clem and I had great sadness in our lives. This could not be denied. But there was something about spending time with him that made me feel like fighting, in a healthy kind of way. We were fighters. I was angry that he lost his little girl, and I was never angry about anything. There was something to rejoice in this, like I had finally reached a stage that I was supposed to have gone through and never did.

And I was hungry, literally hungry. I had a hankering for a hamburger. *Hankering, such a Clem word,* I thought. I couldn't get his way of speaking out of my head. It was plain English, for God's sake, but he spoke it like no one else I had ever met before. Yet he felt familiar.

I remembered seeing a country bar and grill not a half mile from Clem's, and it wasn't long before the Country Inn Bar & Grill came into view. Although "Inn" was part of the name, I was fairly certain that the word had been used loosely, with the sole purpose of evoking charm or country quaintness. Judging from the size and look of the place, it seemed pretty clear that overnight accommodations were not possible. The facade, white clapboard, practically lined the roadside, and the windows were framed with black shutters that were bolstered by cheerful, but obviously artificial, potted plants. I didn't know much about plants and flowers, but—being that it was early November—I was pretty sure that these were red carnations of the synthetic variety. That's not to say, however, that they didn't have their own perky charm.

The bar was cool and inviting. As dark as it was, there was nothing threatening about it. I was greeted immediately by the bartender, who wore a crisp, white shirt, black tie, and a warm smile. "What's your pleasure?" he asked.

"A menu and a chardonnay," I replied, returning the smile.

I hoisted myself up on a wooden stool halfway down the empty bar and began flipping through the day's notes. I couldn't help but feel good. I was surprisingly excited about a book project I wasn't sure would go anywhere.

The bartender arrived with the menu and the chardonnay. Beads of condensation were already forming on the glass, making it all the more inviting. I took a sip, savoring a taste that was fruity and oaky, and silently saluted Clem. I thought we had accomplished a lot in just a few short hours. I had never written a book before, but there was something about Clem's warm, encouraging personality that made it all seem possible. In my mind, I could already see him on the cover, offering the reader a whole barrel of McCouns, his apple of choice. And since it involved strictly his region, we could call it *Clem's Cider Banks*.

I took another sip of the wine as I mulled over a vast assortment of burgers, but before I could settle on one, an unnerving sensation came over me. I was being watched. I slowly turned my head to the top of the bar, the part that had been hidden from view upon entering. The light pouring in the window behind him made it hard to see, and it took my eyes a second to adjust. There was a veil of cigarette smoke swirling around the face, but when it cleared I could see that it belonged to Finn. He smiled wryly before draining his bottle of beer. "Tommy, I'll take another one when you have a minute," he yelled.

"You got it, Finn," Tommy called eagerly from the other end of the bar. My eyes met the words in the menu, but my brain didn't focus.

"El, wasn't it?" Finn asked. I looked up in time to see him taking another drag on his cigarette, and although I couldn't see his face easily, I knew his eyes were dead on me. I wished I didn't find him so intriguing.

"That's right," I said, watching him tap the butt into the ashtray.

"You're getting to be a real regular, aren't you?"

I didn't know how to respond to that. I didn't know if Clem had mentioned the book idea to him. I wasn't sure if Clem wanted him to know. I wasn't sure if I wanted him to know. It really was none of his business.

"I find myself drawn to the area," I said, wanting to leave it at that.

"Fair enough," he said. I gathered that he sensed I was holding something back, but to his credit he didn't pursue it any further. I wanted to believe that he was being respectful, but perhaps my visits didn't really interest him that much. He turned his attention back to the newspaper, which was sprawled out before him, the ashtray functioning as an unnecessary paperweight on the top right corner.

"Why are you so prickly?" I asked.

"It's just my five o'clock shadow," he said, massaging his jaw. I could see creases working into his face as he smiled. He wasn't as uptight as I had previously thought.

"I mean, why are you so angry? Why are people angry at you?"

He didn't answer either question. We were like verbal sumo wrestlers, he and I, each positioning ourselves for the grip that would finally satisfy our curiosity. He tapped his cigarette butt into the ashtray again. I was never a smoker, but I had a feeling that there wasn't a need to do that so soon again.

"I like that you use words like *prickly,*" he said.

The door creaked open, and a slender, petite woman walked in. She glanced my way, but not for long. She immediately turned into the alcove at the top of the bar, knowing that she would find him there. This was clearly an established routine. It was silly, but I was crestfallen. She was not like the woman I had seen earlier at the farm. This woman couldn't be dismissed easily. She wore clothing that was perfect for her body type. She seemed sensible, ready for a cold night. She wore what I believed to be a bomber jacket, and I had always thought they looked great on women of a shorter stature. And she had suede boots to match the jacket. Her jeans were tight enough to reveal her shape, but they weren't painted on. She seemed comfortable with herself, and I didn't have that. I walked in with it, but it was gone now.

In my mind she was the adult version of Una Hinchcliffe. Una Hinchcliffe was my classmate in the sixth grade, and she was a model of perfection. Every sixth-grade girl wanted to be Una Hinchcliffe. She was nice to everyone, and she was certainly respectable, but there was this underlying raciness about her that attracted the attention of every cool boy in the class. She wore hosiery while the rest of us were still in knee-highs, and she had a pair of really cool wedge shoes, neutral in color, the kind that never really went out of style. I could hear Julie in my head, *Trust me, honey, they went out of style,* but in my mind there was something timeless about them, and Una, too, for that matter.

Finn immediately folded up the newspaper and unrolled a few bills from a wad he had pulled from his pocket. Throwing them down, he yelled, "Tommy, I'm taking off. I'll see you later."

"Take care, Finn," Tommy called out from the back.

The woman was already walking out the door when Finn looked my way. "See you next time, El?"

"Next time," I said, nodding. As I watched him leave, something occurred to me. I never had to tell him my name. He had remembered it. He had met me halfway.

Chapter 9

Distress

"What is this called?" I asked, fingering a patch of worn, faded denim on the rack at Bloomingdales.

Julie diverted her attention for a precious lunch-hour second, which was generous. Stolen moments at Bloomingdales were sacred to her. She glanced over to see what I was referring to, her fingers taking a break from a blazing piano dance through the clothing racks. "It's distress," she replied, without having to give it much thought.

"Figures," I said.

"What do you mean?" she asked, turning back to the clothing.

"It's just funny. The apple farmer has this son, and he wears jeans just like this, only I get the feeling his distress is natural, from years of wear and tear, and the irony of it all is that this particular fashion statement, distress, as you say, is the epitome of who he is. He is distress, he causes distress ... he's just a boiling pot of distress."

Suddenly there were no hangers sliding across metal frames, and I could see the fur hem of her black coat swishing toward me. I looked up to see her face in all its wide-eyed intensity, the freckles on her nose dancing with excitement. Her finger rose through the air like a spire as she declared, triumphantly, "Aha!"

"What?" I asked, feigning innocence. I had actually been avoiding any mention of Finn for a while. I knew it would result in a scene like this, but I suppose I was ready to make him a known part of my visits to Cider Banks. She already knew all about Clem. Heck, she even knew about Nanny and Pru, but for a while I had been reluctant to mention Finn, knowing that she would make more out of it than there was.

"I knew it! My gut feelings never betray me. And to think you had me doubting myself! Tell me more."

"Jules, I barely know him. I'll admit that I want to know him, but not for the reasons you think. Don't forget, he experienced a loss like mine. I just want to talk to him about it. I don't know why, and maybe it's a big mistake to think that it would do either of us any good ..."

"Oh El, sweet El, guys don't want to talk about that stuff. You can talk to me about that stuff, or Katherine."

"It's not the same, Jules. Katherine lost her future. You lose a sibling and you've lost a piece of your past."

"How 'bout support groups for siblings?"

"I'm not good in groups. I'm much better one-on-one, and with him there's no group stigma. It's not like I would have to perform at a given time, like 7 p.m. Wednesday nights. If we talk, we talk. No pressure. I don't even need to know that he'll talk about it. The possibility of it makes me feel good. Does that make any sense?"

"Sure it does," she said, placing her arm around me, guiding me over to another rack. "But you know what makes a heck of a lot more sense to me right now?" A smile began to play on her mouth. "Sprucing up your wardrobe. Trust me, ya gotta go with me on this. Now, I know what you're thinking. That Jules, she's so shallow ... she can't even go deep for a second. But that's where you're wrong, Ellen Bannister. Your ol' friend here sees the whole picture. You want to have intellectual chats with him. Fine. I get it. The way to a man's soul is still through the hootchie," she said, slapping my ass.

And that's the way it would always be with Jules. She would never think you could just be friends with a man. It's an age-old debate among women. You either believe it's possible or you don't.

Before I could argue, she had me in the dressing room trying on a variety of blue jeans, all of them distressed. Most she dismissed as soon as I opened the door. There were a few she had to consider for more than a couple of seconds, then saying, "No. Getting closer, but no." There were some that made it as far as asking me to turn around before she cast her final judgment. The winner: a pair of low-riding, boot-leg cut jeans. I knew she liked them when she bothered to walk toward me. "Bend over," she demanded. I quickly glanced over at the dressing room attendant, who was watching us like we were in a third act on Broadway.

"Jules, they're fine. Let's just get them," I pleaded.

"Bend over," she said, using a tone that indicated she wasn't going to ask again.

I could feel half my backside drop out of them as I did, but my worn cotton panties wouldn't let me down. As soon as she saw them, Jules snapped the faithful elastic waistband against my skin, saying, "What's with the granny panties?"

The attendant made a lame attempt to muffle a laugh and left. "They're comfortable," I protested.

She had me stand up straight again, and she walked twenty feet away so that she could take me in from a distance. Then she jumped in the air like a child. "You got yourself a pair of hootchie-mama jeans!"

"What does THAT mean?" I asked.

"It means that if you've got a quarter in your back pocket and you're standing all the way across the room, I can still tell ya whether it's heads or tails."

"And this is a good thing?"

"Get dressed and meet me outside."

☐

When I got outside she was waiting for me at the cash register, twirling a couple of thongs around her pointer finger. As I approached her I said, barely audibly but firmly nonetheless, "I don't do thongs."

"I couldn't live with myself if I didn't at least try." In her other hand she held out a package of string bikini panties. I looked at her hesitantly. "I swear they'll offer coverage right up to the top of your crack," she said. As I pulled them from her, she checked her watch. "Jesus, I have to go. That old witch Clara relieved me today. I'll see you back there." She spun around halfway between me and the escalator. "Tomorrow, boots!"

A reluctant smile played on my mouth as I watched her walk away. I had to admit one thing. As well as the bottom half of my ass, my hootchie-mama jeans seemed to embrace my new philosophy about taking risks.

Chapter 10

Driving in Head First

Due to inclement weather, Julie's weeklong efforts to infuse my wardrobe with style and grace were for naught. Saturday morning I donned my old blue jeans and laced up my faithful Timberlands. I wasn't that disappointed. While I liked the things we bought during the week, they seemed impractical—and frankly a bit silly—for a day of pruning, or for any other type of activity on an apple farm for that matter.

It was 5 a.m. and I stood by the window with a mug of coffee in hand, watching the garbage truck consume bag after plastic bag of Manhattan's refuse, reflecting on a week of unpredictable turns. On Monday I called Clem to make sure that I could stay Saturday night. "Is it okay with Pru too? ... You'll be sure to tell her I'm coming, won't you?" I was pretty sure he would. He seemed on top of things like that, and being that they no longer had that many overnight visitors, I figured he would remember to mention it. I kept thinking about the way Pru embraced me so freely. If she hadn't, I would have probably felt the need to talk to her directly.

Then on Wednesday I had a call from Dorothea Fredericks. She would call every few months to order some more copies of her book, her one-hit wonder, and we'd end up having these great talks. She liked to call right before 5 o'clock so that she could say a quick hello to Julie before she left for the day. Julie didn't have time for a lot of people—the automated answering machine was often turned on before it was technically five—but Julie had a soft spot for Dorothea. Most authors called for sales figures, but Dorothea never did that. I guessed she knew how well her novel sold from her royalty checks, and she wasn't the type who needed to talk about it. She seemed more interested in having a heart-to-heart.

Dorothea never accepted the "I'm fine. How are you?" type of conversation, the superficial kind where it really didn't matter how you were. There was something philosophical and unconventional about her approach to talking.

My first conversation with her had been pleasant, and I had hung up in quiet awe, thinking *Holy Moly, I just spoke with Dorothea Fredericks, the most renowned recluse of the publishing world.* Then I processed her order and, for the most part, put the conversation out of my mind. I had no way of knowing she'd start asking to speak specifically to me. The second conversation was nothing short of bizarre. She had asked how I was, and my response had been my standard "I'm good, thanks. How ..."

"Prove it," she had said, before I could ask how she was.

"Excuse me?" was my response.

"Prove that you're good."

"Uhm ... I'm not sure exactly what to say to that."

"Speak the truth," she said. "Don't worry, I won't hold it against you."

"Okay, I've had nasal drip all day and my marriage sucks, and that's just the prelude to this sad story."

She had laughed heartily, the kind of laugh that used to accompany women saying "Oh darling, oh silly darling" in old black-and-white movies. I was at first uncomfortable and then a bit annoyed. My tone had turned testy too. "Was it books that you wanted, Dorothea?" I had asked.

"Oh don't be like that," she said airily. I waited for more, not knowing whether I could relax and soften just yet. "It's just that I get so tired of meaningless inquiries," she said.

"But you asked me how I was first. You said, 'Ellen, how are you?'"

"Tut, tut, tut, tut, tut, tut. It wasn't a meaningless inquiry. I really wanted to know, and you weren't giving me the truth."

"Because I have a job to do, not to mention the fact that I like being perceived as a professional. I can't take such liberties, you know, to be honest." I had instantly regretted saying the last part, the part about not being able to be honest. Who likes to admit that they're ever dishonest? "Unfortunately that's just the way it is in any kind of business," I added, lamely.

"I never want it to be that way in our business, the business that takes place between you and me."

"Dorothea, what on earth are you talking about? You don't even know me."

"And I never will if you hold to that attitude."

"Well how are *you*?" I had asked, still on the defensive.

And that was the rocky point on which our relationship began. We made a commitment that day that we would always speak the truth to each other. I wasn't sure at the time how long our agreement would last. And since this was all about being honest,

I had told her as much. Inevitably we got to know each other, and pretty well.

So, of course, when she called on Wednesday I had given her the update on Clem and my upcoming stay on the farm. I told her I was going back for the third visit that weekend.

"Where is the farm?" she had asked.

"Cider Banks."

"Cider Banks, New York?"

"Yes. You know it?"

"That's only about twenty minutes from me. Come have lunch," she had said nonchalantly.

"Are you kidding? That'd be like getting to know you all over again. It'd be weird." As I said this, I laughed, thinking *God, I really have gotten honest with her.* When I was met with silence, I added incredulously, "You can't be serious."

"Oh, but I am."

After seven or eight years of brutal honesty, I could sense a deep smile on her face. I knew she was entirely serious.

"Look, we have a pretty good thing going here, okay? It's like a little therapy session every couple of months, free of charge, mind you. It's like having Terret's Syndrome, for God's sake, without being ostracized. You can't buy what we have. And you're ready to put it in jeopardy?"

"You mean to tell me if you were blind and you were suddenly given the opportunity to see, you'd turn it down!"

"Uh yeah, not exactly the same thing."

"Well aren't you a load of crap. Here you are going on and on about broadening your horizons as a way of paying tribute to John, as a way of bettering yourself, and you don't even have the gumption to meet me in person. I never pegged you as a hypocrite."

"Okay, okay. Ouch! But be careful what you wish for, Lady."

"It won't change anything, Ellen," she had said.

I glanced down at my kitchen table, which wasn't in my kitchen anymore. I developed a fondness for eating at the window, and since I have only one window—and my kitchen comprises one wall—my kitchen table is part of my living room now. Next to the directions to Dorothea's house lay the other surprise of the week, a third letter from Clem. I picked it up and traced a finger along the triangle of the unopened back flap. The paper was nice to hold, the usual high-quality stock. Opening it would betray him, I thought. Things were different now. I knew him now. He knows me. He thinks he writes to a stranger. I put the letter back down next to the directions so that the two dilemmas of the week were side-by-side before I turned my attention back to the window, took another sip of coffee, and watched the sun come up on a new and already unsettling day.

☐

The directions called for me to make a left onto Crooked Hill Road, which, true to its name, was full of blind ascending turns to the left and to the right, intermittently. The deep brush at the side of the road made me feel as though I had fallen into a canal. It swept against mounds of compressed soil, the buttress for the strongly rooted trees that towered over, I guess, Crooked Hill. It came as no surprise that an unyielding terrain led to the door of Dorothea Fredericks.

I had butterflies, of course. I kept saying her words over in my head: *It won't change anything, Ellen.* The house had no number. There was no need for a formal address, she had told me. There were only two houses on Crooked Hill. I would pass one on the right on the way up, and then hers was the one at the very top. I was nervous, yes, but excited too. I couldn't help but smile as I passed the first house, a homely one, in need of a good paint job, with a pleasant porch and rocker. I continued up the hill until the road merged into a circle of trees. I went in through the right and wrapped around to an old wooden, single-story dwelling of simple construction. The wood appeared dry and worn—you wouldn't want to light a match too close to it—but the house had charm. It was an old country cabin, the kind that would take offense to any method of updating.

I got out of the car, slamming the door behind me, hoping the bang would draw her attention. When it didn't, I took a deep breath and climbed the three or four steps to the porch. Again I waited. When she still didn't come out, I crossed the porch with ginger steps. Stability was not my friend at the moment, whether due to nerves or the questionable condition of the porch was debatable.

Face to face with the door, I raised my hand to knock, but before I made impact I heard a latch lift. The door creaked open and there she was. She had aged well. The poofy brown hair, now shades of salt and pepper, had been cut into wispy tufts that framed her delicate facial features and reflected her breezy nature. She wore a smoky pink sweater of loose, light fabric that fell to a fashionably uneven hem just below her hip. A teal blue boa was draped loosely around her neck, the fabric of which I'd be hard-pressed to identify. She was a vision on a cloudy day, outwardly defying the season with her pants of white denim and her rosy rouged cheeks.

I took another deep breath. "I'm just going to speak to you like I would on the phone," I said. "That's what I'm going to do."

"Good."

"Well, am I what you expected?"

"Better," she said quickly, her smile lines, rippling up both sides of her cheeks, adding immense character to her face. "There's actually a lot of promise in you as far as your appearance goes," she said, stepping aside to let me in.

I released a laugh. "Well I can see you're going to talk to me just as you would on the phone too!"

"I told you nothing would change," she said, knowingly, with a smile. I took a moment to study her, to visually compare her to the picture that hung on the wall at Burke & Patterson, the one that, at least in retrospect, made her seem like a caged animal to me. Her eyes were still intense, yes, but there was a coolness, a sureness, a confidence, an all-knowingness inside them now.

"You've changed a lot," I said.

"What, from that picture you tell me about?" she said, shutting the door. "I should think so. That was twenty years ago."

"In a good way," I said quickly. "I mean, you aged well. I guess that's what I'm trying to say."

"There was nowhere to go but up really."

I had been surprised to learn in an early phone conversation with her that the photograph was taken at arguably the lowest point in her life. I remember feeling like a talk-show host when she told me. "Wait a minute," I had said. "You mean to tell me that you were somewhere in your mid thirties, you've got this hit book on your hands—and "hit" is pretty much an understatement here—and you weren't happy?"

"Strange, isn't it?" she had replied.

"I mean, it's the stuff people dream about. What more could you possibly want?"

"Apparently it's not for everyone. I'm living proof. You never know until you're there. It wasn't the right time for me. I had another journey to take," she had said lightheartedly.

"Do you ever think about the road not taken?"

"Don't we all?" she had said with quickness. "But I've learned not to live long in the what-ifs. It's fun, even natural, to ponder them, but the point is that I'm happy with the road I took. If I can offer you a small piece of advice," she had proposed, letting it hang in the air, or in our case, in the wonders of fiber optics. I had pleaded with modern technology not to fail me.

"I'm listening," I had whispered into the phone, afraid I would miss something if I said anything more than that.

"The grass will *always* look greener on the other side, *if you let it*. Don't let it." Her advice, I learned in the years that followed, was always simple and succinct. But it spoke volumes really, to me at least.

And the road she took? She went back to school and became a nurse. I suppose she was always a healer at heart, and she answered her calling.

She had been surprised to hear about her photograph hanging in the hall at Burke & Patterson when I first mentioned it to her years earlier. And now, here she stood in front of me. She had walked away from it all. Looking at her, I just knew she had made the right decision. "To think how many have looked at that photograph and never known what a low point it was for you." I marveled.

"So publicity wasn't my thing. Thank God I was a quick study on that," she said, laughing.

I turned to take in her home. "Look around, Ellen," she said as she left me. "I need a couple of more minutes to prepare lunch."

It was an open-floor plan, three large rooms merging into one. At the far end of the room was a sizeable dining table, which struck me as odd, considering Dorothea didn't seem the type to entertain. To the right was the living room. She had started a fire, and it was beginning to cast a soft glow on the round glass coffee table in front of it. Above the fireplace was a large oil painting of a sailboat on rocky waters, the black and gray cloud cover ready to cave in on top of it. Four brown wicker chairs with plaid cushions were evenly distributed around the table, like points of direction are on a compass, reminding me that the course of conversation with Dorothea Fredericks was always impossible to determine.

The entire left side of the room was a combination of office and living space, with a table and laptop in the front by the window, cushioned sofa and armchairs in front of another fireplace, and two large credenzas forming the shape of an L in the upper corner of the room, one laden with books, the other providing a lengthy stage for small wooden figurines. The wall above the second credenza was dotted with children's artwork. The frames had been carefully selected to complement the dominant color in each work. Some of the artworks included little notes in crayon. I walked over to read the messages. One was written under a perfectly arched rainbow next to a pair of red shoes: *Dear Nurse Dorothy, Thank you for taking us on a trip to Oz every day by reading to us.* The letters got smaller toward the bottom of the page, but I could still make out the last sentence: *You are no Wicked Witch. Melissa: Age 9.*

Glancing at the others, I could see that they were all addressed to Nurse Dorothy.

"I never thought of you as one with an identity crisis," I called in.

"What do you mean?" she called back.

"Dorothy?"

"It's just easier for the kids to say," she laughed. "They called me Dorothy more often than Dorothea, so I decided to go with it."

"I think you like it," I teased.

"I certainly don't mind it," she laughed.

I picked up one of the figurines, a carved giraffe, as Dorothea entered carrying a serving tray. "From Africa," she yelled over. "You haven't lived until you have visited Africa." I put the piece back down in between a carved elephant and hippo.

"You were there on safari a couple of years ago, weren't you?"

"Safari and then some," she yelled as she reentered the kitchen.

She came back with another tray, and I followed her to the glass table. "In most parts of Africa people are grateful for what little they have, and in many parts if they have something as basic as fresh water they feel lucky. But look at us, look at what we have before us," she said, coming up for air. "Now that's a broccoli and cheddar quiche," she said, pointing as she spoke, "and that's a spinach salad, a vinaigrette dressing in this pourer, a Caesar in that one. Sliced tomato over here. There's hot water in the teapot, a variety of teas in this box, iced water over there, sliced lemon here … and let's see, what else? I have red or white wine if you like, and I could always make a pitcher of iced tea if you don't feel like hot tea."

"Geez, if I had known you were going to put on such a spread I would have come years ago."

And as quick as a whip she replied, "You weren't invited years ago." She smiled and arched her eyebrow, pausing before she said, "Zing."

"So what's with the ominous painting?" I asked, sitting down.

She looked up at it as she spoke. "It reminds me that life is fragile. And often short." She turned her focus back to me. "It's good to be reminded of that. But who knows that better than you? So where are you now in all of it? Four years later," she inquired, starting in on her salad. I knew she was referring to John.

"I feel good. Especially lately. I feel like lately I've been pushing myself to draw from John's energy, I mean the energy I remember him having, and it is paying off. I guess I'm getting used to not having him around physically, but that doesn't mean I won't talk to him. I find great peace when I talk to him and when I replay memories of him too. I guess it's sort of like prayer. I was never really good at praying. I suppose people who pray find that sense of peace. Don't you think?"

She smiled and nodded, not saying anything. I got the feeling she wanted me to keep talking, and I didn't mind. I was revealing unusual, and deeply personal, information about myself, but it was easy to do with Dorothea. We had plenty of conversations like this after John died, and she was enormously helpful. She is a smart woman, yes. Well read, well traveled. But she has something beyond that, something that you can't buy, something you can't learn from a book. She is emotionally intelligent, and beyond that, she isn't afraid of *being* emotionally intelligent. There are people who are emotionally intelligent, yet they can't direct the gift in a way that it's helpful to others. She is unique in that she can.

After John died, there were those who would dab their eyes with a Kleenex and turn the other way if I mentioned that I talked to John, particularly Aunt Celia's friends. They always meant well. They always inquired how I was doing. Their hearts were in the right place. But they also made me feel, unintentionally, that mourning him in this way was something I should be embarrassed about. Dorothea wasn't afraid of discussing loss, and ways of mourning, or anything that I considered meaningful. She wasn't afraid of hearing whatever I had to say. With Dorothea there was freedom.

"I like to think that he's still out there, and proud of who I'm becoming, proud that I don't shy away from letting people into my world anymore. Don't get me wrong, I don't pull people in from all directions either. I haven't become a kook. I'm just expanding my comfort zone and embracing who and what comes my way."

"That's terrific, Ellen," she said, still smiling. "And tell me, who has come your way?"

I knew what she was getting at. She knew why I was in the area, and I knew she was looking for the latest information on Clem. I actually wanted to talk to her about him. I pulled out the latest letter, still sealed in the envelope, and slid it across the table. She picked it up, saw that it was unopened, and looked at me questioningly.

"I can't bring myself to open it, although I'm dying to know what's inside," I told her. She all too quickly handed it back to me. I had hoped she would analyze the handwriting, ponder every serif, and consider the possibility that the letters could reveal something about the true nature of the man.

"Why won't you open it?" she asked.

"I know him now. It would be as invasive as opening his diary."

"It certainly would not," she laughed. "It's addressed to you, for God's sake." She paused for a second before speaking again.

"Did it ever occur to you that he might realize that you are you?" she asked.

"What do you mean?"

"You know … that you, El, are indeed Ellen. And what on earth does he think your last name is?"

"He never asked. It's never come up."

"That's just it. Don't you think that's odd? He may know you somehow, from someplace. He may be totally on to you," she said with the wave of her hand. She settled back in her chair and cocked an eyebrow at me. *Damn, I wish I could do that.* She looked at me intently as she took another sip from her mug. I could still see the curl of her mouth behind it. She did, indeed, enjoy stirring the pot.

"No. No way. I used to think that he might know me somehow. I remember considering that when we first met, but now … no. I don't think it's possible. I don't think he could. I don't think he's capable of being that coy. He's …" I struggled to convince her, searching for the word. "He's … genuine," I said, pleased with myself for pulling a bit of John's sass from up my sleeve.

"Okay. How much longer are you going to let this ride out though? When are you going to tell him that you're Ellen Bannister? The one he writes to!"

"I don't know. I have to admit that I do feel like a bit of a weakling. In the beginning I kept telling myself, once I get to know him I'll tell him. I thought it would be easier once I got to know him, but it hasn't worked out that way."

She offered a chuckle of amusement, but nothing more.

"Well?" I pleaded.

"Well what?"

"Advice please! You always have plenty to say! Where are you now, when I need you?"

"You want advice? I think you should tell him, and soon. I would need to know if I were you. The curiosity would eat me alive. I would want to know, I would *need* to know, why he writes to me. But it doesn't make a bit of difference what I think. You won't do it until you're good and ready. And that's okay. It's your situation, not mine, and if you need more time, then so be it." She slowed the pace for a minute, still thinking. *Good, don't stop thinking,* I thought to myself.

"I'll tell you something else too," she said. "There's a part of you that doesn't want to know why. You *need* him. You *need* something to happen in your life, something away from Burke & Patterson, something away from that studio apartment you coop yourself up in, something away from everything you ever knew about yourself. You didn't like what you saw in yourself. Something was missing. Nothing felt meaningful after John died. And you didn't want to waste another minute in a life you considered mediocre at best. And good for you, Ellen. You did something about it. Good for you. And now, you found someone that you can relate to, and you don't want to lose it. The closer you get to him, the more there is at risk. But guess what?" she asked, leaning over the table now, both eyebrows arched this time. "There is something you haven't considered. I'll bet money on it. Yes, you've come a long way, but you're still overlooking a valuable part of the equation. He needs *you*. Yes, that's right. He needs you too. Imagine that. Pound for pound, you may actually pull more weight here. But, no, that would never occur to you. So tell him. Things may actually be better once you do."

After she spoke her peace, she announced that she was getting dessert from the kitchen, leaving me with a strong case to come clean with Clem. I sat and pondered the thought that he could actually need me more. She was right in that I hadn't considered that a possibility.

"And what about men?" she asked, reappearing with berries and cream.

I knew what she meant, but I didn't like making the invasive questions easy for her. It was easy to ask for her advice on Clem. I wasn't so sure I wanted her advice on my love life. "What of them?"

"Any dates lately? Or do you find solace in being the belle of Burke and Patterson?"

"You know, I could ask the same of you and I never do."

"You could, but you won't. It makes you uncomfortable. You haven't expanded your comfort zone *that* much," she said, laughing heartily.

I could feel my cheeks burning, so I decided to take up her challenge. "Belle of Crooked Hill, are you?"

She laughed again, as if she truly enjoyed the jab. She grew serious then, but she spoke warmly. "I loved once," she said. *God damn, she really wasn't afraid to tell it like it is.* "And it was all I needed. Enough to carry me through my life. I don't look for it anymore. The memory of it is enough for me. Someday, when it doesn't embarrass you, you'll ask me again and I'll tell you all about it."

She took another sip from her mug, still looking at me intently. "So how many others do you think you can fit into your world right now?"

"What do you mean?"

"I can set you up with someone. You're spending time up here now, even staying at the farmer's house. How about a date?"

I started to giggle like a schoolgirl. "What!"

"Come on. It'll be good for you. It'll be fun."

"With whom?" I asked, feeling like a bit of an ass. Even though I knew it was correct to say *whom* instead of *who* here, I felt like an ass, as I always do whenever I say *whom.* It just never sounds right.

"Someone from the hospital. He's head of administration there. Recently divorced. Not real ready to date. Not really looking for anything serious. You're perfect for him right now," she quipped.

"God, I don't know whether to be insulted or relieved that I'm viewed as 'nothing serious,'" I said, curling my fingers into quotes and dramatizing with heavy eye-rolling.

"I didn't say that. I said that he's not really looking for anything serious," she said with a laugh, before turning a little more serious herself. She continued to consider it, holding her jaw in the crook between her thumb and pointer. "He's a little older than you are. He's about 45."

"Seven years older," I said with attitude.

"Last time I checked he was still going out to dinner without the aid of a walker."

"Okay," I said, after a small pause. "You get on that," I said, rising. "I'll leave you with that challenge," I said, picking up a tray.

"That's not all you can leave me with. You can leave me with the clean up too," she said, taking it from me. I picked up the other tray anyway and followed her into the kitchen. "Go have a chat with an apple farmer. I don't want to be used as an excuse for delaying it any further."

I quickly scanned the kitchen as I set the tray on a wooden counter next to the sink. It was as basic as the rest of the house, perhaps even more so. There was an old stove, a small refrigerator, and two yellow vinyl chairs with chrome frames pushed under a Formica-topped table. She had a few potted plants on the windowsill that must have fought hard for the limited sunlight available to them, although they looked like they wanted for nothing.

"Some vegetables from the garden," she said, handing me a brown paper bag so full that the top couldn't be folded down more than twice. "I grow them out back."

"How?"

"How what?

"How do you grow them out back with all these trees everywhere?"

"There's a little clearing in every wood, even a dense one," she said, patting the top of my head a couple of times, then turning to leave the kitchen.

"Hey!" I protested, following after her. "I caught that." She could be so silly.

"Do you know how to get out of here?" she asked, reaching for the latch on the front door.

I started to backtrack in my mind, but she interrupted my mental replay. "No, wait. I have an easier way to take you out of here than those directions. It won't seem as direct, but it'll actually shave a little distance off your trip," she said. As I followed her out the front door, I couldn't help but smile at the mention that it wouldn't seem as direct.

"I want you to follow me. I just have to pull the car out. I'll be with you in a second," she called over her shoulder as she began walking back to the single-car garage at the rear left of the house. The garage door was like a foreign contraption to me, with a handle and crank I wouldn't know what to do with. A little elbow grease and she had the door raised. I admired her independence, her obvious reign over her domain. She knew herself well, and her surroundings suited her spirit. I turned for a second to take in the view from the top of Crooked Hill. In spite of the trees, I could still make out several houses that dotted the hilltops around her. She wasn't quite as alone as a visitor might think at first. She did have neighbors, should she need anyone, although she didn't strike me as the type who needed anyone.

I turned around in time to see the shadow of dense foliage fall over the well-contoured hood of a steel-blue automobile, preceded by a leaping silver feline. As it purred out of the garage, I realized in amazement that it was a Jaguar. I didn't see that one coming. She even had vanity plates, but hers were of a mocking nature. She had R.N. in miniature letters to the left, the way a doctor would have M.D., and then the core letters of the plate spelled out NURSE.

I followed her down Crooked Hill and watched the Jag come to a slow halt in front of the house on the left, the only other house on Crooked Hill. An old, balding man, slumped in stature, slowly made his way from the porch to the front gate. She extended her hand from the car, and he leaned on the top of the gate and reached out to her. They spoke for a minute, with their hands in a comfortable embrace the whole time. I knew their conversation was coming to a close when she leaned out to cup his hand in both of hers. Then she stretched across her front seat and produced a brown paper bag, identical to the one she had handed to me. I could only guess that the contents were the same, and I felt a pang of envy when it occurred to me that a clear difference between me and the man, other than years, of course, was that he was a regular recipient of her kindness.

And as we continued to wind our way down Crooked Hill, I felt somewhat transcended. Dorothea had that effect on people everywhere, I bet. No wonder she became a nurse. She was a healer at heart. When you left her, you felt healed. You felt promise. You felt direction. And like a nine-year-old girl named Melissa, you saw the yellow brick road before you. And you got the feeling you weren't in Kansas anymore, or the vicinity of Cider Banks, or anywhere else earthly for that matter.

Chapter 11

Direction, Literally and Figuratively Speaking

There wasn't much daylight left when I arrived on the farm. I had called Clem to tell him of my plans to meet an old friend, and he knew I was coming on the late end of the afternoon. He was thoroughly unfazed. "Have a good visit," he had said. "I'll be here when you get here." And there was nothing passive-aggressive about his response. He meant it. But now I felt a little panicked about the work that lay ahead. Other than his brief tutorial, I had no prior knowledge of pruning, and I wasn't sure how long the job would take us.

I pulled up to find him on the porch, relaxing with a mug of tea and a newspaper, which he read by flashlight. Two identical pairs of shears and canvas gloves lay on the table in front of him. His reading glasses sat halfway down his nose and he elevated his gaze to meet mine. He smirked as he said, "I thought you'd never get here."

"Am I too late?"

He glanced in the direction of the setting sun as he rose and pocketed the flashlight. "Honey, I've always been one to believe it's never too late, but even I have to concede that there are only so many hours in a day. It's us against Mother Nature now." He picked up the shears and gloves, hobbled across the porch, and swung his arm around the porch post for a little torque before leaping down to the soil. All I could think was that he must have done that move a million times over the course of his lifetime. I didn't know anyone who lived in the same house his whole life, and the idea of knowing a place so well fascinated me. "Let's go get her," he said. I was ready to suggest that tomorrow was another day, but his momentum made it clear that he enjoyed a race against time. "Come on," he said, and I began to trail after him.

"How'd it go with your friend?" he asked, as we walked into the early twilight.

"It was great. I never met her before, and it felt like I had. That almost never happens."

"You never met her before?"

"No. We became friends over the phone."

"I'll be darned. It's funny how friendships start sometimes."

"Yep," I said, thinking Dorothea would be nudging me in the ribcage right about now, saying *Here's your moment. Seize the day.* I gulped hard, ready to tell him that he had a crucial role in how our own friendship started, when he began to talk of the work at hand.

"On the older trees we use chainsaws," he said, motioning to fully-grown trees in an orchard to the right, "but you and I are going to work on the little guys."

"Here," he said, passing me a pair of shears as we walked. "These are your pruners. You might as well get used to the feel of them."

They were about three feet long and heavier than they looked. "A bit clunky, aren't they?" I asked.

"You can't do what we have to do with a set of nail clippers," he quipped.

We walked a good distance before we came upon a patch of orchard with younger trees, and he surveyed the first tree in the row, circling it and peering into the branches at the same time. Then he selected a branch, grasping it for leverage just above where it met the leader, and snipped it off. The shears snapped as if it were a clean break, but he continued to snip at some small threads of wood until the cut was to his satisfaction. "Ya ready to give it a try?" he asked.

"I suppose it's now or never."

"Put these on," he said, taking my shears from me and handing me the padded canvas gloves. The gloves were a little big for me. "They'll do for now," he said. "We're not going to be out here much longer anyhow. Any darker and you might cut your hand off."

"Now that's a pleasant thought," I said, clapping the gloves together. He handed me the shears and indicated which limb he wanted me to prune, but then he stood back, out of my way, probably afraid to be any closer.

"Go on," he said.

Even though he had just demonstrated what he wanted me to do, I didn't know where to put my hands. It's different when you're doing it yourself.

"Now grab it at the crotch."

"The what?" I asked, a twinge of disgust fluttering in my stomach.

"Oh for God's sake. You're not going to castrate it … Jeeeezus Christ," he said, apparently realizing what his word selection conjured. "You know, the heel, where the branch meets the leader." I couldn't help but feel my own limbs grow suddenly weak with laughter and I bellied over, conscious enough to hold the shears away from me as I did so. "Jeeezus Christ," he said, turning his head from side to side in a show of disbelief and amusement all at once. After he gained some composure, I had to too. He certainly made room for humor, but I got the feeling that he had only so much room for it when anything to do with apple farming was at hand. "Like we talked about last time," he reminded me. "Like I just showed you."

I opened the pruners and positioned them just as he had, at the heel, as I preferred to think of it, and winced as I applied pressure. "Now that you have placement, you can use both hands if you have to," he said. I could hear the snap before the pain rippled through my hands like a wave.

"Man, that smarts!"

"I know," he said, laughing. "I was hoping the gloves would absorb a little of the shock for you. You get used to it though." He came over to examine the cut. "You done good," he said. I stood back to inspect my work while he raised his own pruners to the area. "Then I usually clean it up a little, since it's never a clean break."

I stepped back and watched him with my palms facing up to the sky in a traditional yoga pose, hoping the air would absorb some of the shock.

"You want to try again?" he asked. I pruned two trees with him that day, the second while he held a flashlight for me.

"I guess we'll have to do the rest tomorrow," I said.

"I already did the rest. I just left these last two for you."

"Why?"

"It's a lot of hard work. You can see that now. I just wanted you to get a feel for it. You can at least describe it now if you have to, right?"

"I know, but I feel like I'm not really contributing anything. I'm not really helping you."

"Don't worry. We're not entirely finished yet."

We walked by flashlight back to the house. "Are ya hungry?" he asked.

"I'm as full as a tick. I want for nothing after the feed I had."

"Good food?"

"Yep," I said, appreciating the memory of it for the first time. It felt good to be around people like Dorothea and Clem. We walked quietly the rest of the way, his flashlight guiding us like a terrestrial beacon.

☐

It was fully dark by the time we got back to the house. Clem had prepared a makeshift library on an old draft table in the barn. For light, he used an oil lamp that looked to be right out of *Little House on the Prairie*. "Aren't these dangerous?" I asked, picking the lamp up to determine its weight and stability.

"Well you don't want to forget about it. That's for sure."

"Why are we out here?"

"Are you cold?" he asked, his voice cracking with considerable concern.

"No, not at all," I said, only then considering the temperature. It actually felt great. The air was brisk, and my cheeks were numb. It was rejuvenating. I felt like a child again, as if I had been out playing in the snow for hours and I didn't want it to end. "It's not the temperature. I was just thinking ... wouldn't it be easier to look over all these books inside?"

"Are you kidding? With Pru and Nanny in there? Heck, they'd be interrupting us right and left."

"Oh, okay," I said. "No, this is fine. I actually like it."

"The oil lamp was my father's. He used to work out here a lot. Now I find myself out here a lot too. You know, you eventually end up like your parents, I suppose," he said with a laugh. "You spend your whole life fighting it, but in the end you pick up plenty of their traits."

I didn't feel like telling him that I would never know if that were true or not. I had wondered many times about how much of my mother and father I had in me. I used to worry that I would never know myself very well because I never knew them very well. Those thoughts always ended the same way, with me quietly hoping that I wouldn't be like Aunt Celia.

I remember John saying once that the most important thing in the world was to be known well, even if just by one person. I liked the idea of this. It always stayed with me. I like it even more now. Most people think that it's important to know others well, and of course it is, but there's no line of connection if you can't let them know you. I remember saying to John that it seemed like a self-serving idea, the need for people to know you. He said, "On the surface it seems selfish. Why is it so important to be known?

But if you don't share yourself you're just looking at the world through a porthole and never really going anywhere."

Of course John was that one person who knew me well, who made sure I knew that I made a difference, that the world was a slightly different place because I live and breath. I could hear him in my head: *People need to know they make an impact.* After he died I felt as though my relevance to anyone had died too. But then I kept hearing him in my head, as clear as I heard him in the car that day he took me for my road test, calling to me again and again, the same line over and over: *You might want to take a ride someday.* And it had nothing to do with learning how to drive.

I started thinking—maybe because of people like Clem and Dorothea—that it's not over for me. I could let others know me well too. Just because I didn't know my parents doesn't mean I don't have roots inside me, doesn't mean I don't have experiences to share. It could make me eternal if I did. Because John let me know him so well, I'll have him with me forever. I can let others know me well. This is something I have control over. This is something I can still achieve. We're probably all fighting for this. *The important thing to remember is that it all starts with you, Ellen Bannister.*

"El, you with me?" The sound of Clem's voice woke me from a dream world.

"I'm here," I said with a fright. I was startled and embarrassed.

"I was just telling you about the oil lamp, and I lost you."

Then it hit me like a ton of bricks that this conversation of parents was best to be avoided until I told him who I was. I didn't know how much he knew about me, me being Ellen Bannister as opposed to me being El *whatever*. Dorothea had me thinking that he may know me somehow, and I didn't know if he knew that

119

Ellen Bannister's parents were dead. Sure, I could have told him right then and there who I was—that would have made sense—but the idea sprung up on me too quickly. It was actually perfect timing in light of my discussion with myself about sharing things, but I wasn't prepared the way I had been in the orchard. I was still coming out of my dream world. My nerves were getting the best of me. So much for sharing! I rotated on my heel, trying to stay calm, looking for something, anything, to ignite a different topic in my head, when my eyes fell upon something every bit as disconcerting as the conversation. He had started working on the motorcycle. There it was, propped on its kickstand, do-it-yourself books splayed across the floor. Wrenches, screwdrivers, and tools I didn't have names for fanned out from the books. He had told me about his daughter's death when we visited the historical society. It was okay that I knew that much, but I wasn't supposed to know that it was this motorcycle, the one he kept in the barn. That was in a letter. It was getting more difficult to keep straight what I should and shouldn't know.

"I thought we'd cover fertilization today," he said, flipping through the pages of one of the books.

All I could think seconds earlier was how monstrous a space the interior of the barn was, and now all I could think was how tight the air felt around me, how the walls and roof might as well have been right on top of me, how the entire structure had just been dwarfed by life and death, from the very beginning to the very end.

"Fertilization?"

"Yeah, fertilization," he said nonchalantly, again with his nose in the book. "There won't be anything substantial to show you out in the orchard for a few months, but we can cover the whole cycle right here," he said, knocking his knuckles on the wood of the table. "Come on," he said, looking up from the book. "What are ya waitin' for?"

I walked over, not knowing how long it would take me to focus on what he was saying. It was hard to get the image of the bike out of my head. To me it represented his greatest life struggle, and it was pressing up against my back. *How did he not feel it too?*

□

He spoke about fertilization as if he were reading poetry. Every line sounded melodic. Every detail of the process seemed crucial, actually was crucial. It was as if apple tree fertilization had something to do with the beginning and end of the world. I got the feeling from listening to him that he would quickly perish if he left the orchard for long. His tutorial was mesmerizing, so much so that I completely forgot to take notes. It would have been pointless to do so. Only his own words, verbatim, would serve justice to how beautiful the process was. Spoken by any other mouth, it would all seem rudimentary. I was convinced of this. The lesson was positively hypnotic. When he shut the book it was as if he snapped his fingers and an unwelcome invitation to return to reality had arrived.

Although the book was now closed, I got the distinct feeling that the lesson wasn't entirely over. He stood there with his worn, bumpy fingers gently tapping the leather-bound cover before finally casting his eyes my way. "El, I was hoping you could help me with something." He grabbed the oil lamp and hobbled away from the table and toward the motorcycle, toward death itself. I found myself saying, *Ellen, stay away from the light.*

But he could not be ignored for long. "I've been working on this old bike, trying to restore it to its former glory, but it's hard when the person trying to repair it has seen better days himself. I was wondering if you could hold the flashlight for me for a few minutes." He turned around to look at me, an uncharacteristic bashfulness playing on his face. "My eyes would be grateful."

"Of course," I said, feigning eagerness. How could I refuse him? I'd go to the ends of the earth and back for him, but I didn't necessarily like the request. I wasn't sure I wanted to see him on the bike, but on the other hand I knew it was something he needed to do.

He handed me a large flashlight and told me where to position the light. "Now just hold it right there. This shouldn't take more than a couple of minutes."

I watched him work the ratchet in quarter turns until the first screw came loose. He referred to one of his manuals and then turned his attention to the next screw while I found the lapse in conversation deafening. I kept thinking that if I didn't know his daughter had died on this particular bike I'd be asking him all kinds of questions about what he was doing. That was the type of relationship I had with him now. I felt comfortable asking him almost anything. So in an effort to be myself I asked, "What happened to the bike?" *Easier to ask about the bike than the rider,* I thought.

"Not really sure," he said matter-of-factly, straining to work the second screw out of some rust. "We'll never really know for sure. Best picture we can make out of it all is that Judith must have leaned too hard into a turn."

He said this as if I had already known that Judith died on the very bike in front of us. *Did he know who I was? Did he know he had already told me about this bike in the letter?*

"Roads were a bit slick. Tires could have been newer. The only visible skid marks were her own, so it's unlikely she was avoiding another vehicle. She could have been avoiding a squirrel for all we know. She hadn't been on the bike in years. Not really sure why she got up on it at all. I suppose everybody wants to turn back the clock once in a while, relive a bit of their youth." He smiled up at me.

We were quiet for a while, and he continued working. After several minutes, the handle bars fell loose and he quickly gripped them tightly with his hands so they wouldn't drop to the dirt floor. That's exactly when he told me the bike belonged to Finn. That's exactly when the tight grip on the bars meant more to me than fixing the bike. *How he'd love to be able to hold Finn that tight. How he'd love to be able to steer him in the right direction.* That's also when I knew I wanted to really look at the bike. It was a Honda Rebel 470. *Figures,* I thought. I didn't know anything about motorcycles, but it didn't surprise me that Finn would have a Rebel. I moved closer to where Clem was working so that I could look over his shoulder at the manual.

It was around this time that we heard footsteps making their way through the graveled drive. Clem stopped working. He shot me a look that had *Brace yourself* written all over it, and I suddenly felt my heart beating in my chest. I didn't know what was about to happen, but it didn't feel like it would be good. I was the first one visible to Finn when he appeared in the door of the barn, and I could see a look of playful amusement cross his face for a half a second, no doubt ready to scoff at my apple-farming ambitions, that's of course until he spotted Clem and the motorcycle. Then the curl in his mouth disappeared. His eyes, all joy draining from them, kept shooting from Clem to the bike and back to Clem. Then all the tension of a Western shootout hung in the air like thick smoke.

"It's time for me to do this, Finn," Clem started softly. The words had barely spilled out of Clem's mouth when Finn made an abrupt turn to leave. "I *need* to do this," Clem called after him. "I'm sorry if it hurts you, but I don't have as much time as you do."

I was willing to put money on it that Finn heard every word. I was willing to bet he'd spend a lot of time processing the message too, whether he'd ever admit to it or not. Those words carried too much weight to dismiss. They'd have to stay with him. It was a heartbreaking scene really.

Clem, who was on his knees, struggled to get up. I went over to assist him, but he was a tough old bugger. Whether he saw my hand there or not, I'll never know. He managed to get up on his own. His gait was a little unsteady at first, and I hoped the needles wouldn't last too long, that the blood would rush through his legs and steady him. He hobbled over to the barn door and I followed him with the flashlight still on. If I couldn't shed light on a hopeless situation, then, by golly, I was going to at least make sure he could see where he was going. But he didn't go far. He stopped in the door and watched the silhouette of his son slip into the darkness from which he had come.

We watched what we could see of Finn getting into his truck. We listened to the motor turn over. We heard the tires fight for friction against the loose gravel. And together we followed the red taillights with our eyes until we could see the truck no longer.

We stood for a moment in the cold air, the breath of life slipping from us like puffs of cigarette smoke. Then Clem spoke.

"El," he said in a far-off, dreamy kind of way, not pulling his eyes off the direction in which Finn had gone. "Remember what I was telling you before? Even self-pollinators benefit from a little companionship." Then he turned to look at me. His gaze could not have been sharper forty years earlier. "You understand what I'm saying, right?"

Chapter 12

Discovery

As a result of a round-about request from Clem, within about a half hour's time I was walking into the Country Inn Bar and Grill in my hootchie-mama jeans and black leather boots in search of a conversation with Finn. I expected him to be in the alcove section of the bar, but to my surprise he was seated where I had sat last time, halfway down the bar, his shoulders hunched over, his elbows burrowing into the mahogany, his beer gripped as if his reflection in the glass bottle revealed the answers to the world's greatest mysteries.

The slam of the door behind me attracted his attention, which made me wonder if he was waiting for someone. But then again, more heads turned than just his. There were more people there this time, and I had envisioned it being as empty as it was the last time. His assessment bore into me, a top-to-bottom search for information, and then there was a quick dismissal. I had butterflies to begin with, but now I was truly nervous. I began to question everything about my appearance. I had surveyed myself in a full-length mirror in one of Clem's guest rooms before I left, and I had signed off on my outfit with complete confidence, thinking *Damn, I'm 38 and I still got it.* It's funny how you can feel completely comfortable with the clothes you selected in the privacy of your own room, yet feel like a shrinking violet in the public eye. I steadied myself, which was difficult in my heeled boots, and began walking toward him.

Somehow he sensed that I flanked his side, but he still didn't turn to look at me. "What's up, El? You meeting someone?" It was as if he was talking to the bottle. Just six words, and I was happy and sad simultaneously. It always made me feel good when he remembered my name, but I can't fully explain the sadness that washed over me simply because he thought I might be there to meet someone. Someone else. It's as if it never occurred to him—or didn't interest him—that I might be there to see him, and for some reason that bugged me. You would think it would bolster my self-confidence that he thought I had a bit of a social life, but instead it made me feel lonely. And maybe a bit embarrassed. Embarrassed because I wore my hootchie mama jeans and the boots with a heel and I wasn't there to meet anyone but him.

"Can I sit here?" I asked, motioning to the stool next to him.

"It's all yours," he said.

"I'm not meeting anyone," I began. "I was actually hoping to find you here." This got his attention, and he halfheartedly turned. "I was hoping we could talk," I said.

"Yeah? About what?"

Tommy approached with a menu, but I placed my order right away—same as last time, a burger and a chardonnay—before I did my best to answer a difficult question. "I don't know your father that long, but I hope you don't mind if I say that I care a great deal about him."

The barstools weren't the type that swivel, which made his sudden twist a surprise. "So older men are your scene?" His ambivalence disappeared and there was a sudden coldness in his voice. It took me a second to process what he was getting at.

"What? It's not like that. Obviously not." I looked at him in disbelief and waited for something. I'm not sure what. An apology maybe. I just know there was a long pause. "That's disgusting," I finally said, hearing an unforeseen terseness in my words. And then there was regret, for there was nothing disgusting about Clem. "I mean, it's not disgusting … I don't mean that. I can't even entertain thoughts like that about your father." I could feel the anger welling in me. "I resent that I have to convince you that I have no interest in him in that way. This is such a stupid and unnecessary conversation. What is wrong with you?" I spurted.

"All right, down girl. Take it easy. Just take a second to see it from my perspective." We were both quiet for a minute and then he continued. "You're like this mystery. No one really knows why you're here." *Did he just call me mystery? Did I just hear that?*

"Does he wonder why I'm here?" I was worried for a second. "Your father, I mean. Does he wonder?"

"No." I could feel myself breathe again as Finn took another mouthful of his beer, taking his time to swallow hard before he continued. "He never talks about you. He wouldn't though. He's not … he doesn't have a cautious nature." He turned his hardened face to me. "He's trusting."

"It's not always a bad way to be."

"He welcomes everyone and everything that comes his way. I look at you and I wonder why you're here."

"I'm writing a book about apple farming."

"You may be writing a book, but you're here for more than that. You need something, and I'll be damned if I can figure out what it is." He took another hard swig from his beer, I was guessing more to buy time to gather his thoughts than out of a desire to drink. "He told me about the book after your first visit, but I didn't think you'd come back. I only needed to lay eyes on you once, and I knew you weren't a woman interested in writing a book about apple farming."

I couldn't understand why he was so sure. But he was right, of course, which frightened and delighted me at the same time. It was like I was known, which was a bit of a relief. He somehow knew something about me, and he had no way of knowing for sure. I thought about telling Finn why I was there. For a second it seemed like a good idea. It might ease his mind about me. It might tell him something about his father he needs to know. But about a second and a half later I knew I couldn't betray Clem. "At some point in your life you will have to trust someone too," I said. "There isn't a malicious bone in my body. Your father is very endearing. It doesn't take long to care about him."

"Don't get me wrong. I didn't say there was anything *malicious* about you. *Malicious,* now that's a strong word," he said, shaking his head. He turned completely around to face me. "Just not forthcoming," he said, his eyes piercing.

"Look, El, before this goes any further, I want to set you straight on something. I love my old man, okay?" His eyes were eating into me now. "If that's what you need to hear, I've said it. You can leave right now if that's what you came to hear. If you were looking for drama ... there, now you have it. You say you came here to write a book about apple farming. So go ahead and write it. Just don't make domestic strife your specialty, okay?"

There was nowhere to go but to be utterly honest. There was no room for anything else. There was no room for any layer of intrigue. There was no room for coyness. I didn't want him angry with me, and all I could think was that he would see through anything less than honesty. Anything less than honesty in its purest form would fuel a raging fire in him and engulf me in such a way that I could never come back again.

I sucked in air and began to let the words tumble out. "I'm not a drama queen. And if I had the slightest idea of what a happy domestic life was, I wouldn't be sitting here right now. I wouldn't need to come here, and that's the God's honest truth. And I'm not looking for a sympathetic ear either. Although that might be nice once in a while, I'm certainly not looking for that. I have friends that can give me that. I don't need you for that. But I care about your father. I would have liked to have had a father like him growing up. But you, you don't realize how good you have it."

Everyone there got quiet for a minute. Only then did I realize how loud I was. My eyes were stinging and my cheeks were flushed, and I got up to leave. He grabbed my hand quickly, which frightened me at first. "Don't go." And for a moment I thought I detected something desperate about those two words, but if there was he pulled it together quickly.

"Just hang on a minute, okay? Don't just go. Okay?" His grip softened but he didn't let go. "It doesn't have to all spill out at once, does it? I'm the angry one, remember?" He laughed a little, and his thumb actually stroked my fingers before he released my hand. He stretched his arm around my back so that he could pull my barstool out and then he gestured for me to sit back down. The atmosphere began to fill with voices again. He must have known half the people there, but he wasn't embarrassed. He acted as if they weren't there. "I want to listen to your story," he said.

I wasn't used to being angry, so the scene was a big deal to me. He must have seen it too, because he kept saying, "It's okay. Just take your time. Okay?" I took a deep breath. "And whatever you do, don't run out of here." He hung his head low like Clem does sometimes. It was the first time I noticed something similar about the two of them. "Don't let me upset you." Then he looked up again. "I just don't have a filter sometimes, okay? I want to hear your story. I want to hear what happened to your father."

"I know what happened to your sister," I said. He was expressionless, just waiting for me to go on, just waiting for me to say more, as if I could fill him in on something he didn't already know. I kept thinking that I didn't want to waste time anymore. That was why I brought her up. *You want to know my story,* I kept thinking, *yeah, well, my story is sort of like your story.* Wanting to have had a mother or a father was surely part of my story, but the truth is that I couldn't remember enough of my parents for them to have had a big part in molding my story. *Losing John is my story.* "I know what you're going through," I said.

"All right, hang on right there," he said, his hand going up like a stop sign. "If we keep this about you, I'll listen, but I hate it when people claim that they know what somebody else is going through, particularly when that somebody else is me and they haven't the slightest idea."

"No, I do. Sort of. I know every death is different … I'll allow for that … but my brother died suddenly. So you can't say that I don't know what I'm talking about because that's simply not true."

Seconds of silence felt like an eternity, the bait to my everything dangling in front of him. *Will he take it?* "What happened to him?" he finally asked.

It was strange telling him how John died. For the longest time I felt like the whole world knew. I told Julie, and then Julie had already told everyone at work by the time I went back. People would call on the phone and not mention it, and I can remember wondering if they knew. When they didn't mention it I would eventually say things like, "I don't know if you heard, but my brother ..." And then they would stop me. "I know ... we know ... I'm so sorry." Bad news travels fast, so I never really had to tell anyone but Julie and Brian. Brian was the only person I actually remembered telling. So in a way it felt as though I was saying the words for the first time. "He was pushed off a subway platform."

Finn just kept looking at me, stone-faced, not saying anything, so I added little pieces of information to fill the silence. "EMS came, but there was nothing anyone could do. They said he died right away."

"How long ago?"

"Four years."

More silence. "Only sibling?" he asked.

"Yeah."

"I'm sorry." The sorry came quickly, with no emotion. He wasn't looking at me anymore. I kept thinking that it would have been easier for him if I had had issues with my father. He shifted on the stool a little, applying more pressure on his elbows for a second. He was clearly uncomfortable, and I wasn't sure if he'd choose to engage in any further discussion on the matter.

I just kept talking anyway. "I can still see him in my head, as vividly as I could the day he died. Isn't that funny? I've heard people say that they can no longer see the finer details of the deceased's face anymore and that it scares them. Maybe because I look at his picture all the time I see him in my head as if he's standing before me. No one could make me laugh the way he could."

And then I laughed out loud. I couldn't help it. It had been so long since I talked to anyone about John. I'll always share how I'm doing with anyone who asks, and if it's somebody real close, like Dorothea, I'll speak about my new mission, my mantra to explore new things as a way of honoring him. But after a while, after a few years, I didn't like to go on about specific memories anymore. But with Finn, all the memories were fresh again, and this topic of sibling loss was all I knew that I had in common with him. But it was huge, so big it filled up the bar and the small section in the back full of tables, and crept up the tables for two that lined the windows behind us, even sweeping up into the smoke that veiled the air between us and the ceiling. I released one of those laughs that escapes from your mouth the way a housefly escapes from a stuffy room once a window is finally cracked open. In fact, before the sound escaped I didn't know if I would laugh or cry. It came out as laughter, but inside it felt like a mixture of the two.

Then my heart jumped in a beat of panic, and I looked to see if this was a source of amusement for him. Or worse yet, if he pitied me. Or maybe he would pick up the bar napkin that lay in front of him and dab at the ketchup that had gathered in the corners of his mouth, the male equivalent of Aunt Celia's friends going at their eyes with their handkerchiefs and their tissues, just so that he wouldn't have to look at me anymore. But he *was* looking at me, and it was neither a look of amusement or pity. He was right there with me, waiting for me to go on.

"What about your sister?" I asked. "What happened to her?" It wasn't really a fair question of course. In part because he had already told me he didn't want to talk about it. And the other part, of course, was that I already knew part of it. But I was desperate to hear it from his perspective.

He turned away and there was silence again while he stared down the lines of bottles on the other side of the bar, the tops reflecting off the mirror behind. I looked at them too. There were only two rows, but with the reflection in the mirror it looked like their tops formed a sea of lost souls staring from a shoreline into a deep, dark abyss of unknown. He'd swim right in if he could, I thought. If it meant he could get away from me. Bet he was a good swimmer too. He could make a clean break for it. But I'm sure he couldn't help but see what I saw. We were in there too, just beyond the bottles were our own reflections. There was no escaping us really.

Suddenly I was fancying the bottle tops as a line of defense, a marching army. *We're bigger,* I thought. *Together we could take them.* I wasn't inclined to think that he would share my perspective, and I was trying to think of a detour when he gave me an invitation to go on. "Four years isn't all that long ago, is it?" he said. "Bet you still think about him all the time."

It was just a small step. I shouldn't have been that relieved. I didn't know if he could talk his way through a conversation like the one I wanted to have with him. I started taking shallow breaths of air so that he wouldn't notice that I had to gain momentum for speaking. And then as soon as I started talking, I lost myself in it anyway. It's like that when there isn't room for anything but honesty. You don't have to think too hard about what you're saying. I started to tell him what it was like for me.

"I remember in the beginning thinking that five minutes of my waking life couldn't go by without my thinking about him. Now I wonder if an hour goes by without him coming to mind. I'm sure it must, maybe even two here and there, but he's never far from my mind. He's always going to be right around the corner from everything I'm doing, from most everything I think about. And that's okay with me. I want it to be that way. He's part of the reason I'm here, in Cider Banks I mean.

"It's like his death opened a door to myself that I didn't know was there. I never knew that the words he spoke to me regularly would eventually have this effect on me. They didn't until he died. That may sound morbid or self-centered, I know. Believe me, I'd shut the door to myself again to have him back. I'd live half the life I could. But there is no going back. You can only spend so much time entertaining thoughts like that. So I push myself to go forward. He always wanted me to try new things, go different places. It's my way of honoring him. I always say to him, 'Here I am, John, trying new things, just like you always wanted me to.'

"You think he knows?"

"I know he does. It's a feeling I have. I feel like he hears me when I speak. Do you feel connected to your sister like that?"

He had wanted me to keep it about myself, but once I started to explore loss I wanted to know how everyone else dealt with it too. The initial silence that followed made me nervous, but when I looked at him I got the feeling that he was putting effort into what he was going to say, that he was searching for honesty too. He looked pained, but at least not angry.

"I used to think it was possible. I had some experiences in the beginning that made me feel like she was with me, but I don't think so anymore."

"Why not?"

"I don't know. You know, I used to think I would see her."

"*See* her?" I asked.

"Yeah, *see* her."

I remember really looking at him while he took another sip from his beer. I was searching for embarrassment, but there wasn't any, which I thought was a wonderful thing.

"And then I read somewhere that Freud believed that such sightings were part of a hallucinatory wishful psychosis, and I stopped thinking it was possible that I had any real connection to her beyond my memories."

"Freud said that? He actually used those words, *hallucinatory* and *wishful?*"

"Yep," he said, surrendering it all to Freud.

"How dare Freud! How ignorant of him!"

"Is he now?" Finn said, laughing incredulously. "You just called arguably the greatest psychoanalyst of all time ignorant. Are you aware of that?"

"Not only ignorant, but insensitive. People *want* to believe that they are still connected to loved ones that have died. This, of course, is true. It's what keeps people going. I understand that, but who is Freud to suggest that it isn't possible? And Freud, not being dead himself when he said it, would not have been in a position to know whether it's possible or not." I took a sip from my wine and tried to stay calm. "It's not like it hasn't occurred to me that I could be imagining things here and there simply because I miss John so much. I have thought about this. I'm a very analytical person, actually. You'd be surprised. But the more I think about it, I keep coming back to the same conclusion."

"What's that?"

"That the circumstances that surround my experiences could never merely be coincidental."

"All right," he said, palms open, fingers beckoning. "Give me one of your experiences." He was enjoying this, but he was respectful too.

"Okay," I said, mentally sifting through a trove of them, trying to pick one that had a lot of persuasive power. "I took a photography class when I was in college. One of my assignments was to do a portrait where I was to highlight a particular feature of someone's face. I always envied John's eyelashes. They were extraordinary eyelashes," I said, taking another sip of wine before I continued. "Long and thick, every girl's envy, so I knew right away that he would be my subject, and that I would make him sit for a portrait in profile.

"I liked the photo I took, but I wasn't proud of it technically. It was too grainy, but I gave it to John anyway and I never saw it again. After John died, Katherine, she was my brother's fiancée, and I were at his apartment going through pictures, trying to prepare a collage of photographs for the wake. She came out of the bedroom laughing, holding an 8-x-10 black and white that she had pulled from a drawer. 'We have to include this one,' she said. 'It's one of the few we have of him with a beard. He absolutely loved this photograph.' I took the picture from her and was stunned to see that it was the photograph I had given him fifteen years earlier. He had kept it all that time. He never told me how much he liked it. After the wake Katherine had it matted and framed for me. It hangs on my wall to this day.

"So about a month after John died, I was looking at it on the wall intently, remembering that my goal had been to capture the length of his lashes. There was nobody in the apartment with me. I was just talking to him, telling him what the plan had been when I was looking at him through the lens. It was very quiet and warm. The light above the portrait was shining on him, and I had an intense sureness that he was listening. I was telling him how important it had been to capture the length and plushness of his lashes. When I was finished talking, I put my fingers to my lips and transferred a kiss to his lashes. It's kind of silly when I think about it, because I would never be so tender with him when he was alive, but I suppose that's the way it is after you lose someone.

" Anyway, none of this is extraordinary, I know, but then I turned off the light above the picture and went to turn on the TV. I watched the image on the screen come slowly into focus. It was a black-and-white portrait of Elvis Presley in profile. It was an amazingly intimate photo of him, a headshot, and the photographer, who you could not see, was speaking, saying how it was his goal to capture the length and plushness of Elvis's lashes."

"Get out!" Finn exclaimed.

"Yes!" I said, thrilled that he seemed to think it was beyond coincidence. "And I know I wasn't watching that channel when I turned the TV off! What do you think of that?"

"I think if you want to see it as a sign you should."

"I do see it as a sign, but don't you too?"

"El," he said, shrugging his shoulders, "I honestly think you could see a lot of things as a sign if you really wanted to."

It shouldn't have mattered to me that he seemed skeptical. Why did I care? Why did I need him to believe that it was possible? He must have noticed that I was crestfallen. He actually took my hand in his for a second. "El, it shouldn't matter what I think. You believe what you want to believe. Is it possible? Sure it is," he said, offering a deep, serious nod, like his father. "I just can't say that I share that confidence. At the same time I don't want to be responsible for taking anything away from your experience."

I had stopped looking at him, but peripherally I could see him slouching to get under my gaze. I reluctantly looked at him, since he seemed to be waiting for that, and he began speaking again. "I don't want to take anything away from the inner peace you so clearly have. That's a wonderful thing. So don't worry about what

I think." Then he released his grasp, leaving my hand cold again, the dampness of doubt working its way into the bone. *Don't let yourself be so fragile,* I thought.

I flipped through the files of my memory again, needing to challenge him, needing to challenge myself. "I have another story too."

"I'm all ears," he said.

"Are you sure?"

"Absolutely. Go ahead."

"After John died there were two names I kept hearing him say in my head, names he had either mentioned to me in conversation or names I had heard him say when talking to someone else. Maybe both. I had never met these friends of his before. One of them was not a name that would easily roll off your tongue either, so it was noteworthy to me that I kept hearing it in my head. I sought these two people out. I asked Katherine to introduce me to them. She was able to find one of them, Tony Orslany, at John's funeral. The other, although I heard he was there, eluded me. The wake and funeral passed and still I never met him. Tony, however, became a very close friend to me and to Katherine. In fact, Katherine, Tony, and I did everything John was supposed to do, attended every function he said he would be at, until we ran out of things, until we ran out of plans that John had made for himself.

"John died in June, but he had made a prediction just a few days before he died that the Diamondbacks would beat the Yankees in the seventh game of the World Series. It was just this strange prediction, strange for many reasons. John was a Mets fan, so why was he thinking about the Yankees? And the Diamondbacks were a young, mediocre team in June, so why would anyone think that they were going to win the World Series the following October? Tony said John told him he saw it in a dream. Tony said John was beside himself with laughter when he told him, poking Tony in the shoulder with his finger, saying, 'You mark my words. The Diamondbacks are going to take the Yankees in the seventh game of the World Series this year. I just have a feeling about this dream.'

"So the end of baseball season arrives, and low and behold, who's in the playoffs only the Yankees and the Diamondbacks. At that point Katherine and I said to Tony, 'What are we supposed to do if they go to the World Series together?' Tony said the plan was to watch the seventh game at Triumph, but to hold our horses, that we were a long way from a World Series seventh game between the Yankees and the Diamondbacks. But Katherine and I got all giddy with every game anyway. Then they both advanced to the World Series, and we allowed the suspense to bubble inside us like lava in a volcano. I think Tony was sorry he said anything. I think Tony thought that his words could be every bit as destructive as a volcano in the end. Katherine and I just wanted to believe that something wonderful was possible. I guess we wanted to believe that between life and death, there will always be the inexplicable, the stuff that is almost unspeakable, the stuff that somehow keeps you going. We were riding on whatever that was.

"We were looking for a sign, I'll admit it, and I've come to learn that you should never look for signs. It's cruel business, and nine out of ten times you'll find yourself taken. But this one wasn't one we conjured up. This whole crazy idea came directly from John, directly from him, and it was our last place to go where we knew he would have been, and I suppose we just wanted to feel him in the air."

"So what happened?"

"Sorry," I said, laughing, "I don't stray too far from the relevant facts, do I? And *you* musn't be a Yankees fan, 'cause you'd already know. The Diamondbacks beat the Yankees in the seventh game of the World Series."

"That did not happen," Finn said, all stone-faced, making a declaration rather than asking a question.

"Yeah, it did."

"It did not."

"It did. The Diamondbacks beat the Yankees in the ninth, 3-2, in the seventh game of the World Series."

"That's not what I mean. I believe all that, but you're telling me that your brother dreamed up the outcome of that game in June, and in October it happened?"

"Yeah," I said, and even though I had only been a girl scout for a few months in the fourth grade, I held up my fingers and added, "Girl Scouts' honor. Or I swear, or whatever it is you need to hear me say to believe me. And I'm not even finished with my story yet. That's not even the part that hits me in the center of my chest. Remember how I was saying that there were two people that I wanted to meet, two people that John had told me about and I knew I had to meet them?"

"Yeah."

"Well as soon as we saw that Diamondback cross the plate in the ninth inning, we were completely drained of all energy. You would think we would have been off our stools doing happy slappies, but we were nowhere near being capable of doing that. We were emotionally spent. The whole bar was emotionally spent, but for a different reason. It was full of Yankee fans, saying, 'Fuck this,' and 'Fuck that.' But the three of us, huddled together, just kept looking at each other like we had just seen a ghost, and in a way we had. We couldn't speak to each other. There was nothing to say. Finally we took our drinks off the bar in unison and quietly clanked our glasses together at knee level, where no one could see them, allowing our minds to drift where they would.

I started to think about how grateful I was to Tony, how I never would have known any of this only for him. Then I started to think that Katherine must be thinking the same thing. And then my mind drifted to the other person, the one I never met, Chris Birchovsky. John used to call him Birchie. So I'm sitting there thinking about Birchie, passively wondering why he was the other name I kept hearing in my head, thinking the only way this could possibly be more complete aside from having John with us would be if Birchie were with us. Then my eyes catch the name Chris Birchovsky on the television screen. As I'm reading the name to myself, Tony gets up off his stool and starts pointing at the TV screen, yelling, 'There's Birchie.'"

I looked at Finn and took a deep breath. Suddenly it didn't matter to me that Finn see the possibility of a connection between life and death. I knew I did. Every time I think of that story I know I'll feel the same way.

I was tired after telling Finn the two stories, tired in a good way, tired the way you might be after running a marathon. Aching, but so alive. There really is only so much you can say. You either believe that there's a connection or you don't. I had come to learn that it was a very passionate subject for me, and it would probably be better, for me and for others, if I didn't try to wrap my beliefs around everybody else. I took another sip from my wine and looked over at Finn.

"Pretty powerful stuff," he said.

We were quiet for a minute. I was happy to be with him, happy there was respect between us. And I was resting.

"I'm going to hunt Tony Orslany down one of these days. Make sure you're not fibbing." I shot him a look, but I could see a smile pulling at the corners of his mouth as he drained his bottle.

"You do that," I said quickly, finished with my rest.

He ordered another round for us. I was glad, because I didn't feel like leaving. It felt good to be reflective, and I wanted to stay for a while.

"I remember reading once that it's the most underestimated loss there is, losing a sibling," I said. "People forget that in all likelihood the sibling relationship will be the longest intimate relationship of your life, often twenty-five or thirty years longer than your relationship with a husband or a wife, often a whole other lifetime after the death of a parent. You're counting on it to be long."

It was becoming clearer to me that if I paused long enough, he would eventually speak. So I waited.

"I'd agree with that," he said, rubbing his chin.

I continued to wait. I watched him pick up the chilled bottle, and I was sure I detected the dampness seeping between his fingers. I felt bad for him. I wanted nothing about him to be cold. Still I said nothing. *Wait, El. Easy now. Wait for him.* It was hard to see him struggle, to run the risk of awkwardness that so often comes with silence, to watch years of hardship pulling at his face. I kept reminding myself that it would be a grave disservice to him if I spoke too soon. His reprieve would only be temporary. *Give him a chance to speak, for God's sake.*

And then he did, slowly at first. "I always thought that Judith and I would bury my father together." I watched him smooth away the bottle's condensation as he spoke. I was so grateful he was a pensive creature, that he took the time to replay thoughts,

143

that he was willing to revisit them. *I would wait forever for you to speak,* I thought. "I must have been preparing for that day at least a decade," he continued. "Had a recurring vision of us standing in black at the gravesite. It was easy to do. It didn't require a lot of imagination on my part, since I know exactly where he's going to be buried. He and my mother bought a plot for four when she got sick. She had said that life would determine who, if anyone, would occupy the additional two spots, but having two children of her own it was unthinkable to her not to have a plot for four."

He turned to look at me. "That was her exact word for it, *unthinkable.*" He turned his face from me again, his thumb pulling back the corner of the bottle's label. "Eventually I stood in the exact spot I had envisioned, only it wasn't Judith I was standing next to. It was my father. I remember thinking *THIS is unthinkable.*"

"Exactly," I said, feeling a bit stupid that I couldn't think of anything to add to it. We sat in silence again for a while. And then I asked him, "Do people still ask you how he's doing all the time?"

"All the time."

"When you lose a sibling, people always ask how your parents are doing," I said. "I suppose it's only natural. In my case, I had to tell them that my parents were already deceased. I always wondered why they didn't then ask how I was doing. But they rarely did. It was as if a sibling couldn't possibly experience sorrow on a level anywhere near that of a parent's. That seems to be part of it. And that may be true. Not being a parent, I wouldn't know how accurate that assumption is. But I still find myself screaming in my head, 'It sucks from a sister's perspective too!' The other part of it is that I suppose the inquiries are always easier if the people involved aren't in the room. So they never turn to me by default and say, 'Oh, okay, then how are you doing?'"

"I don't care if people don't ask how I'm doing," he interjected. "I don't want them to know how I'm doing anyway. I don't need their sympathy. But you're right. They ask about him constantly. I haven't the foggiest notion how he's doing. But imagine their surprise if I told them as much? I act like I know the answer. I tell them, 'He's managing, thanks.' Keep it as brief as possible. It's not like he tells me how he's doing. It's as if it never occurs to people that we don't talk about what happened. How am I supposed to know how he's doing? The damn motorcycle has a better idea how he's doing."

"Why does it bother you that he works on that?"

"He thinks of it as a resurrection. He thinks he'll feel better once it's fixed. There's no fixing this. I'm not interested in pretending with him."

"I don't think he thinks of it that way."

"Yeah, he does."

"No," I said, shaking my head. "I don't think so. I don't believe that's it at all. In fact, I think his fixing the bike has a lot more to do with you than with him."

"Me? Okay then," he said, turning to face me. "Care to share how?" He was a bit flippant, but more tolerant than he had been earlier.

"I think he thinks it will help heal you."

"Heal me?" he asked, disbelievingly.

"Yeah, heal you," I said, wide-eyed, hoping my eyes could drill it into him. "Help you live again."

"El, you above all people should know that there is no healing here."

"I disagree. There's no fixing it. I agree with you there, but healing can definitely take place. Why don't you help him with the bike?"

"Help him kill himself?" And he looked at me just as he did that first time I met him, his eyes like steely blue daggers. He looked at me as if my mind couldn't think within the realm of reason.

I took a deep breath, getting ready for what I had to ask him. "Why are you so angry, Finn? What's that about?"

He wrapped both hands around the barrel of the bottle as if in prayer, one thumb resting on top of the other. "He didn't tell you about it?"

"No. Not too much anyway. It seemed like there wasn't a lot to say. After a while there just isn't a lot to say about a tragic accident, I guess. The details don't seem to matter after a while. The outcome is still the same."

"He didn't tell you that I was the one who restored the old thing?"

"No."

"He didn't tell you I left the keys in the bike that morning?"

"No."

"She asked me if she could take it to the store. I left the keys right there for her. She hadn't ridden the bike in years. Said she thought it would be fun. I never even stuck around to make sure she'd wear the helmet. When we were kids we rode without one all the time. We used to let our hair fly in the wind. What was I thinking? I just thought she knew."

"She didn't wear a helmet?"

"No, she did."

"Then why are you beating yourself up about it?"

"I'm just trying to explain to you that I didn't give it a lot of thought. I didn't really take the time to look out for her," he said, all hushed, like it was a secret between the two of us.

"She was a grown woman. She knew what she was doing." I wanted him to think about what I was saying, to take the responsibility off himself, but he continued forcefully.

"It's bad enough that I had something to do with her death. Now he wants to fix it, ride it himself, and then I'll be responsible for his death too."

"You can't blame yourself for your sister's death. That'd be like me blaming a deranged individual for John's."

"Don't you?"

"No," I answered quickly. "The truth is I don't think about that guy a lot. I feel sick when I do. I remember asking the detectives about him. I know he was emotionally disturbed with a history of mental illness. That's about all I can remember, and that's about all I wanted to know about him."

We were quiet again, but the silence was fueling a need in me to explain myself. Perhaps I wanted to prove to him that I wasn't betraying John by not prosecuting, by not hating his killer. "He was deranged," I said. "If I wanted to blame someone I suppose it would be the system, but what's the point?"

"So it doesn't happen again. Changes should take place so that the same mistakes don't keep happening again. That's what I'm getting at here. If I kick my heels up enough maybe he'll realize that fixing that bike isn't something he should be doing."

"So they get more stringent about letting mental patients leave their facilities? So they say 'No' to more people who may be ready to start building a life for themselves? Everything has its price, Finn. Mental illness is so little understood. And before I go sounding like too much of a saint, the truth is I don't have the energy to be an advocate for much. I don't want to spend my time fighting a political battle when it's not at all clear to me how much good would be gained from it. It suits some, but it's not for me. I don't want to spend my time being angry. People used to tell me that it was a stage of grief, that I'd wake up one day and be angry about what happened, that it was a stage I would just have to go through. They used to have me believing that I wouldn't recognize myself for a while. Finally I decided not to worry about it anymore. I guess what I'm trying to say is that everything has its price. Guess I was one of the lucky ones. I don't carry any guilt, but I guess I still have some pangs once in a while. Don't you ever get tired of it, Finn? Don't you just want to let it go sometimes?

"I'm sorry that this conversation has become so convoluted. I feel like we're going nowhere," he said. "And I definitely don't want that."

"Can you understand that prosecuting that man was something I couldn't do? It wasn't part of who I was, and it's not part of who I am today. I want that to be okay with you."

"Of course it is."

"So you can allow me that?"

"Absolutely, El. I never meant to imply that you should have handled it any other way than how you chose. It was the right choice for you, and I totally get that."

"All right then, I'm going to take a big leap here. Don't be mad at me, but I think keeping your father off that bike isn't saving him from anything. It's killing him. Your way of protecting him is conflicting with the way he needs to handle it."

We were quiet again. There was a lot to think about. "I'm sorry I got off the issue of the bike," I finally said. "I get defensive sometimes about the way I handle John's death."

"El, I don't even know you very well, and I already have no doubt in your love for John. People would have to be stupid not to see it."

"Can you give yourself the pardon you're so willing to give me?"

"That's a tall order, El."

"You must know, in your heart and soul you must know, that you are not to blame for this. You had no way of knowing what was about to happen. You have nothing to prove with this anger. And if you think your father blames you, then let me give you the same pardon you just gave me. I don't need to know Clem any more than I do to say with complete confidence that he doesn't blame you. In your own words, Finn, there is no fixing this. There is just accepting it for what it really is."

"Tell me something funny that John did," he whispered after a minute, softness in the words. Weariness too, or was it the hint of resolution? He loved to listen. I loved to talk. I was happy to offer whatever escape one more story had to offer, but the question caught me a bit off guard. Although my memory ran deep with such stories, it was difficult to come up with any quickly. I ended up going with the first one that came to mind.

"After we both moved out," I started, "we'd go to Aunt Celia's on Sundays for dinner. Aunt Celia was a tough, tough woman. Tough to please and tough to love. We didn't always look forward to the dinners, but we were grateful to her for taking us in, for keeping us together I suppose. She almost always served string beans. One night John was somehow able to maneuver a string bean with nothing more than his tongue so that it lay horizontally across his top row of teeth, spanning not only the two front teeth but the canines as well, and of course whatever ones are in between—I don't know what they're called—but the amazing thing was that he was able to secure it in place and still talk.

"He made sure I noticed first, and then he initiated a serious conversation with Aunt Celia, all the while keeping a perfect poker face. She didn't notice at first, which prompted his facial expressions to become more exaggerated as he spoke. When she finally noticed, she started waving her finger in front of her own teeth in an effort to silently draw his attention to it, the way one might try to alert their dinner partner before he embarrassed himself in front of a table full of guests, only it was just us. There was no reason for alarm, no reason for formality, but yet she couldn't bring herself to tell him that he had a string bean on his teeth. We both knew she wouldn't.

"He went on telling this story, I don't know whether there was any truth to it, but he told it without skipping a beat. She continued to motion to him, until he couldn't possibly not see her. And then he asked her if she was okay, again with such seriousness, the string bean now dangling haphazardly from a couple of teeth. She could finally take it no longer. She rose out of her chair, clutching her fork in her hand, and stretched across the table to remove it from his mouth. John and I just lost it.

"He always took it beyond the point of reason with Aunt Celia. We had a rough upbringing. Don't get me wrong, she never beat us or anything like that. But she would wear you down, beat any enthusiasm you had for life right out of you if you let her. John would never let her."

"Why was she around so much? Why couldn't you just get away from her?"

"We lived with her. She raised us. Our parents died together in a car accident. I was 8 and John was 6."

"You were older than your brother?"

"Yeah, I know. To hear me, you would think he was older, that he was the caregiver, and he was. Aunt Celia was our only aunt. I suppose she did the best she could."

"Was it just the three of you?"

"And Uncle Ed. Poor, sweet Uncle Ed. If ever there lived a kindhearted soul with absolutely no backbone at all, it was Uncle Ed. One afternoon he came in from work a little earlier than he normally would. There was some power outage at the factory, and the employees were sent home early. Aunt Celia was still out, grocery shopping or something, and John and I were doing our homework on the floor. We didn't even look up at first, but then I remember John quickly rising to his knees out of the corner of my eye. 'What are you doing here?' he asked in delighted bewilderment. I looked up then, afraid of the unexpected visitor, only to see Uncle Ed folding his umbrella and slipping it into the stand inside the door. 'Got off early,' he said in a hushed tone. He was beaming. He stepped a few strides closer and bent down to us, his hands on his knees. 'Where's Aunt Celia?' he whispered. 'Out shopping,' John answered quickly, his eyes like saucers.

"Uncle Ed was over the moon about having a couple of hours off. It was gloomy out, but it was as if Uncle Ed wasn't going to let it rain on his parade. 'Do you kids mind if I put the Rat Pack on?'

'The what?' John asked.

'The Rat Pack is a group with Frank Sinatra in it,' I said.

"Uncle Ed couldn't have been more pleased. 'That's right, El. Good for you. They're a very cool bunch of guys,' he said, making his way over to the stereo, which, back then, was a piece of furniture in and of itself. It was like a credenza that took up

151

half the wall. He took the LP out of its sleeve with the utmost care and placed it on the turntable with all the excitement of a child with a new toy. The first song he played was "The Way You Look Tonight." Before long he was snapping his fingers to the beat, becoming a new person, one we never got to see. The melody started to envelope all three of us, and we started swaying around the room. John was surprisingly attentive to the lyrics, and I remember him asking Uncle Ed if the song was how he felt about Aunt Celia, if he remembered a smile that crinkled her nose, and Uncle Ed chuckling and saying, 'Sort of. Something like that.' Even then, John saw possibility in everything. 'Play another,' John begged.

"It was right about then that Aunt Celia took the room by storm. 'What the hell is going on in here?' Uncle Ed quickly went to the stereo and shut it off, a freshly poured high-ball in his hand. 'Ed,' she demanded, 'I asked what's going on in here.' But before he gave her an answer she rushed to take the drink out of his hand.

'Just takin' a little trip down memory lane,' Uncle Ed said sheepishly.

"Poor Uncle Ed. He was 100% sweetness. Never knew how to defend himself. He lived and died by her rules. We all did, and that's the way it was growing up. But John handled it so much better than I did. John brought sunshine to a world that would have been very dark for me without him. He was a good egg," I said, as if this summed him up. Not happy with my analogy, I added, "A remarkable egg. The kind of egg a farmer would hold up in the palm of his hand and say, in a state of deep appreciation, 'Now that's an incredible egg.' You know, kind of the way your father feels about McCoun apples."

"What?"

"You know, McCouns. Your father's favorite apples."

"Yeah," he said, rubbing his chin again, looking like he was replaying a memory in his head. "You know, I had forgotten how much he liked McCouns. I suppose if you had asked me what his favorite apple was, I would have been able to come out with McCoun, but gosh, it's been a long time since he mentioned that."

"And maybe a long time since you've listened," I said impulsively, as if a doctor had just used one of those instruments used to check involuntary reflexes on my tongue instead of my kneecap.

He looked at me, his stubbled jaw hanging, his face lit with surprise. "Is that right, El?"

"I'm sorry, that just slipped out," I said. An hour or two earlier I would have been embarrassed. But I was able to smile at him, confident that he wouldn't hold it against me.

But he dwelled on it for a second, taking a swig of his beer. "Did he say that? Does he say I don't listen?"

"No, he didn't say that, not in so many words. But I can't help but feel that he thinks he's lost you. I can't help but feel sad that you have to ask me questions like that." Then I said probably the harshest thing I said all night. "He deserves more from you." I let it hang in the air for a second too, before I continued. "He needs to fix that bike. He needs to show you how to live again. It's such a wonderful thing he wants to do for you. It'd be a shame to deny him that."

I could suddenly hear Clem's voice inside me, and I stole a line right from him. "I'm one to believe that it's never too late, but even I must concede that there are only so many hours left in a day." And then, leaning into Finn, I added my own twist on it. "Only so many days left in a life," I whispered. Remarkable when I look back on it, because I don't lean into anyone.

□

When we left it was late and snowing. I followed his truck the quarter mile up the road and we parked the cars at the bottom of the hill, as he suggested. "It'll just be easier to walk down the drive in the morning. Trust me on this one." And I did. It was surprisingly easy to trust him.

Before I gave a thought to the heeled boots, I lost my footing on a stone that was moist with fresh snowfall, and next thing I knew I was planted on the ground. It was that quick. There was no time to feel my heart skip a beat, the way it would if you had the time to try to keep your balance. This was hopeless from the get-go, and because it was hopeless from the get-go, there was no real sense of defeat, no embarrassment from arms flailing in an effort to catch your balance. I started laughing. "These lousy boots!"

He started laughing too. "Yeah, I wanted to ask you about the boots. I didn't peg you to wear boots like these. And what about the jeans? For God's sake, you can tell whether a quarter is heads or tails from just lookin' at your back pocket." He went to grab my hand too soon. My body was still weak with laughter and unable to form any leverage. He fell because I practically pulled him down.

"That's what Julie says, but she thinks it's a good thing," I said, still laughing.

"You are the silliest girl," he said, sliding his hand along the side of my face. The placement of his fingers was unexpected, and I stopped laughing almost instantly, stunned that my numbed cheek could sense warmth pulsating from his fingertips. He was still smiling though, apparently oblivious to the fact that my heart was about to pound out of my chest. And about my chest, I could feel the cold air working its way through my unbuttoned coat, and for once in my life I didn't care. My scarf was draped around my neck like it had no purpose, and that was fine with me. His breath was warm on my face as his eyes began to scan my neck. The laughter had stopped and he was no longer smiling, and all I could hear was my breathing.

I just kept waiting for him to kiss me. *I mean that's what he does, right? With the Una Hinchcliffe girl and all the other girls, right?* But he looked at me longer than I thought he would. My breathing was loud, too loud, and I became self-conscious. "You smell like smoke," I blurted out. And that was it. Any spell he may have been under was broken, just like that. His fingers left my cheek, and he rose quickly, taking my hand and pulling me up.

"I'm sorry about the smoke thing. I didn't mean it." He began walking and I felt a sickening desperation sweep over me. "You can kiss me if you want to."

He swung around quickly. "I wasn't going to kiss you." His face sent out a message that made it clear how incredulous the idea was to him. "What makes you think I was going to kiss you?" He walked on ahead of me, glancing back only once. "You know where your room is, right?"

"Uhha."

"Door's probably open."

Then I watched him walk up the hill and past the house. I watched him 'til the light at the side of the house couldn't stretch far enough to illuminate him anymore. I watched him 'til nothing about him was clear anymore. Once again, he was walking into the darkness from which he had come.

Chapter 13

Confessions

"Jules, I think I'm falling for someone."

"Oh joy!" she declared, sarcasm tainting the words.

"I'm serious, Jules." She kept mindlessly gathering books and stacks of reports. "Jules, what's the matter? You've always made me feel like you've been waiting your whole life to hear me say these words and ... well ..."

"Well what Ellen? Come on, spit it out."

"Well, frankly, your blasé reaction is a little deflating."

"It's not all about you, Ellen. You think I hold all the answers?" she asked, bobbing her head up and down in an expectant frenzy, waiting for me to answer.

I thought about that for a split second. That's all I needed. "No, actually I don't." Jules most certainly did not hold all the answers. Very few, in fact. Funny how her opinion always mattered to me regardless.

"You think I know how to direct you?" she asked, her eyebrows arched in anticipation, frown lines burrowing into her forehead.

"Well ... sort of ... yeah, actually ... on matters of the heart you've always had something to say."

"I'm no more capable of directing you than the three blind mice," she said, bursting into tears, releasing a tattered ball of Kleenex from her palm and dabbing it at her eyes. "Go call someone who can be of real help. Go call Dorothea Fredericks. She might be able to help you."

I stood there as baffled as I could ever recall being. Then it hit me. "Oh my God," I said, cupping my mouth in my hands. "You met someone."

"I can't talk about this right now," she said, mindful that someone was getting off the elevator. It was Tom with the mail cart, but he never even looked at us. He slipped his cardkey into the slot and let himself in on the other side of the reception area.

"Jules," I said, my eyes pleading for more.

"I have no idea what's going on with me anymore. I never felt so defeated in all my life. I think I ... ll ... lll ... llllll ... ove someone," she blubbered.

"But, Jules, that's wonderful!"

"No. No, Ellen, you don't understand. He's awful," she said, grabbing my forearm, pleading with me.

"He's ... he's ... ffff ... ffff"

"Come on, Jules. Just calm down and take your own advice. Just, just spit it out."

"It's the F word, okay?" He's ... fat," she said, her eyes pooled with tears, her voice now calm with resignation. She was, as far as she was concerned, stating a pure and simple fact that could not be denied. For all her emotion, the sentence lay there like a beached whale.

"So? You love him, right? What does that matter?"

"Come on. You know me, El. It does matter. I'm shallow, remember?"

I started laughing. "Honey, don't you see? You're not. It never would have gotten this far if you were. That's the beauty of it all."

"Go try to convince some other girl of the beauty of it all. Go call Dorothea Fredericks about the beauty of it all. I can't help you. I can't even help myself anymore."

"Stop suggesting I call Dorothea," I said, pulling a fresh Kleenex from the box that sat on her desk. "I want to talk to you right now, and not about myself. About you," I said, going to wipe the streaks from her face, but she snatched the tissue from me.

"Ellen, you fail to see the point. I don't want to talk about this right now, and maybe never. I'm just going to break it off with him and get on with my life, so please don't ask me about this again."

And at that the center door of the reception area opened and one of the assistants walked through, ready to relieve Julie for a fifteen-minute break, a morning ritual. Eager to get away, Julie grabbed her purse and slipped through the door, mumbling "Thanks, Sal."

And Sunny Sally, as Julie and I called her, stood there, oblivious to it all. "Morning, Ellen," she said, her face beaming.

"Sally, how are you so happy every day?" I asked.

"Oh, I don't know, I just wake up and hear the birds chirping and ..."

Sally failed to realize that I didn't truly want an answer. "I just remembered," I interrupted, tapping the side of my head. "I gotta go. I'll talk to you later, Sally."

I went back to my office and slouched in my swivel chair, my feet taking alternating turns with the task of quarter rotations, my best thinking technique. *What the heck,* I thought, *I will call Dorothea.*

I leaned forward, grabbed the receiver, and dialed the number, which I knew by heart. "Dorothea?" I asked as soon as I heard that someone had picked up.

"Ellen, is that you?"

"Yes. You gotta minute?" I asked, more as an introductory formality than anything else.

"Oh, Ellen, darling, I can't talk to you right now. I don't have time."

"What? You always have time for me," I said, allowing the true nature of our relationship to take over.

"Yes, I know, darling, but I'm in the middle of something. I've got someone here."

"What's with all the *darlings?* You never call me darling."

"Ellen, I really can't talk right now. Listen, are you going up to the farm soon?"

"Yes, the day after Christmas."

"The day after Christmas? Can you stop here on your way up, say around noon? We can talk then. Would that be okay?"

"Sure," I said, just as I heard a male voice from a distance. "Ohhhhh Dot," he called in a sing-song fashion.

"Dot?" I asked in disbelief.

"I gotta go," she said. "See you on Friday." And she disconnected.

"Dot?" I said to myself. "She's anything but a Dot!"

I swiveled around to face the window, searching for sanity in the beauty of a New York skyline. *Good God, have we all gone mad?*

Chapter 14

Christmas Eve

"Good Lawd! Ellen, you here again? It's Christmas Eve, child. Don't you have somewhere else to be? Ain't no Christmas magic here."

Beezie didn't realize that the answer to that was no. No one ever really asks that question unless they think the person has better places to be. "Beezie," I said, turning from the window, "I could ask you the same, could I not?" I had become a master of deflection.

"You know I'm always here Christmas Eve," she said. "You know I always take off Christmas Day. I push through those glass doors at 7 a.m. every Christmas morning, and I'm home by 7:30. Gave them kids strict instructions not to open a gift before I get there."

As selfish as it sounds, I had been looking forward to seeing her. If her kids can't have her for a couple of hours at least I can. Beezie, with all her Southern charm, was capable of lighting up any northern night. "How is she tonight?" she asked, her tone turning serious for a heartbeat.

"The same," I said. "She's always the same." We both turned to Aunt Celia, who was seated in the middle of the room, her hands clutching the armrests of the wheelchair, ready as ever for battle. "Last week the doctor asked me if she was always like this. I told him, 'Sadly, yes, she was always something like this.' He said that he always asks that question because he never knows with Alzheimer's patients. Sometimes you'll see a patient who once had a sweet disposition become disgruntled, and sometimes just the opposite." I looked at Beezie. "And sometimes there are those who stay just the way they are," and we both started laughing.

"I'm glad you find some humor in it. If you don't laugh, you cry, and there ain't no sense in cryin'. I always say, 'Fine if you want to go cleanse the system. Then go ahead and have yourself a good cry, but don't forget to have a good laugh after it's all over. Life's too short. Ain't that true, Miss Celia?" she asked, tucking the blanket around Aunt Celia, knowing fully well she'd never get an answer. But that's precisely what I loved about Beezie. She always brought to mind the bird in one of Emily Dickinson's poems: "Hope is the thing with feathers that perches in the soul, and sings the tune without the words, and never stops at all." Beezie was special. She'd go and get Aunt Celia's dinner, and sneak something out of the kitchen for me too while she was at it.

It was Aunt Celia's seventh year in the home. The first few years John, Brian, and I came together on Christmas Eve. We'd leave early though, and head off for a traditional Italian fish dinner at Cassarini's, an authentic and highly underrated family establishment offering the very finest in Italian cuisine. I was never sure how the tradition started, as we were of Irish descent. I asked John about it once, and there was some silly remark about *fish* and *Irish* rhyming, going well together, followed by "Must there be a reason?" A quiet dinner was the prelude to drinks at Triumph, where we would embrace the lovable regulars as our family. It was easy to do with John. The line between blood relative and friend was always blurred to begin with, but it was entirely undetectable at Christmastime.

I didn't go to Triumph on Christmas Eve anymore. I made a vow that first Christmas after John died that I would never go again on Christmas Eve. I don't know why. I loved those people. I think I was worried that we would never see beyond the obvious, the elephant in the room, the sweetheart that wasn't.

So since that fateful day, I lapsed into having Christmas Eve dinners with someone who didn't know I was there. For a couple of years it was easier that way. There were a lot of things I said I wouldn't do again. Going back to Triumph on Christmas Eve was one of them. I said I'd never see Bruce Springsteen again too, and I probably never will.

Things were changing though. More and more, I wanted to break out of something. The security I once found in saying *never* wasn't there anymore. In the beginning it felt like a tribute to John, but as time wore on I realized that it was anything but a tribute to John. It was against the very nature of his being to set such limitations. I had developed habits, bad ones. They weren't always bad. They once helped contain what was too painful to face. But I was stronger now. I didn't need to run away anymore. I wanted to face things head on.

Over dinner I kept thinking about Beezie busting through the hospital doors every Christmas morning. I wanted to bust through doors too. And more. I wanted to have something to look forward to on the other side. I wanted people to be waiting for me somewhere too. After dinner I checked my watch and realized I could make the last call at Triumph. There was still time before they dimmed the lights. I could bust through those doors downstairs like Beezie does. I could walk with purpose, my shoes click-clacking through the halls of an institution at rest.

Instead I pushed the tray away and walked softly to the window overlooking the Hudson. I could see the silhouetted frame of Aunt Celia's slumped body in the reflection, but once I got close enough I could see through the glass. There was the warmth of Christmas lights glowing on the other side, burning through me, and I knew in my heart and soul that there would be no more last calls on Christmas Eve at Triumph. That day had come and gone. Even the raw, painful days that followed those days had more or less come and gone. My eyes traced the facing riverbank northward, my mind imagining what last calls sounded like elsewhere, my thoughts of future comrades, hoping they would be people I already knew.

But when I got to the doors downstairs I discovered they were automatic, set off by motion. You had to reach a certain point before they would open. Once you reached that point, there was no resistance anymore. They opened for you. They reflected who I was now. A growing, changing being. A woman in motion.

Chapter 15

A Gift of Epic Proportions

Dorothea had barely opened her door when I started speaking. "I can't believe you had him call me."

She offered a wry smile, knowing exactly what I meant. "Well I didn't think he'd call this soon," she said, with a dash of defensiveness, closing the door. "I thought I'd be the one breaking the news to you."

"I didn't know what to say to him."

"Well I hope you said yes. After all, you seemed open to it a few weeks ago. I never would have put him in touch with you if I didn't think you were going to go out with him."

"I said yes all right. I couldn't think fast enough to come up with a polite way to say no."

"When are you seeing him?"

"Tonight. I'm meeting him at some place right outside of Cider Banks called Speed's, which is funny because the whole acquaintance seems so accelerated to me."

"Oh, Mark Speed's new place."

"You heard of it?"

"Yes, he was a head chef at some foo-foo place in the city, but he gave it all up because he wanted a taste of country living. There was an article about him in the *Journal.*"

"Anyway, we're meeting there for drinks and appetizers, and then we're going to *Chez O'Shea* in Portsmith."

"Oo, la-la. Fancy dancy."

"Well, that's what worries me. He's putting an awful lot of thought into a first date, don't you think?"

"He's a nice guy, Ellen. You'll have fun. For God's sake, you're not marrying him. It's just a date."

"I know it seems like I'm making a big deal out of nothing, but you know that feeling you get when you start liking someone and you don't want to be with anyone but that person? It's like I have this sick feeling in my stomach."

"You haven't even met him yet!"

"No, not him. Someone else."

She looked sort of puzzled at first, but then I could see the wheels turning in her head. "Oh dear," she said softly, her hand cupping her mouth.

"What?" I asked, tilting my head to one side, my eyes temporarily darting to the right corners, doing my best to convey a state of utter befuddlement but wondering if I just looked ditsy.

She allowed her hand to fall away from her mouth in what appeared to be a gesture of resignation. "I was worried about this. Come sit and we'll talk," she said, walking away from me.

"No, wait. You wanted me to meet someone. Didn't you? Why does it have to be your friend?"

She turned to face me quickly. "It doesn't. I don't care who you go out with. And I'm a fairly open-minded person, Ellen, but I can't help but think that it would be nice if he were within thirty years of your age. You shouldn't sell yourself short. That's all. There, I said it."

She turned to walk away while I stood there for a second, trying to put the pieces together. And then the picture came into focus. "Oh my God! You think I like Clem! What is it about me that makes *everyone* think that I have no desire to be with anyone unless he's an old man?"

She stood there, speechless for once, watching me with amusement.

"No really, will you please tell me? Because whatever it is, I want to shake it." At that I started jiggling, as if trying to shake a spider off myself. "And there must be a way of shaking it without me having to change who I am! There must be a way of shaking it without wearing hootchie-mamma jeans … or five-inch heels!"

"All right, all right. Calm down. I'm sorry. So my concern was unfounded. You don't have to do a dance to convince me." Her eyebrow rose. "So who are we talking about here?"

"His son."

"His son? You're dancing around here like I couldn't be farther off target! Meanwhile the apple doesn't fall far from the tree, does it?"

"That's corny. And besides, this apple is forty years younger than the tree."

"Sorry, I couldn't resist." She paused for a moment. She was intrigued. "A worthy pursuit?" she pressed, the trademark eyebrow suavely arched as high as the Gateway to the West.

"Not sure yet. I'm not sure what he thinks of me. Most of the time he makes me feel like I'm the one dangling, haphazardly at that, between a worthy pursuit and a worthy adversary. But I suppose I should concentrate on the *worthy* part. That's positive either way, right?"

"Who cares how *he* feels. You know what you're feeling, right?" she called over her shoulder, walking away from me. "Act on it."

"Wait a minute, don't you want to hear more?"

"When you have something to tell I do."

"There was almost a kiss."

"I don't want to hear about almosts," she said, throwing a hand up in the air as she stooped to open a drawer. "You're too young to be thinking about 'almosts.' You think 'almosts' are a big deal? You know what 'almosts' will do to you? They'll keep you from exploring other options, options that may mean you don't say 'almost' so much twenty years from now. Tell me more when you have a story to tell."

I took off my coat and slumped into a chair at a table by the window. She came walking back toward me with a wrapped gift she had retrieved from the drawer. She slammed it down on the table and took a seat kitty-corner to me. The gift, while of considerable weight, was clearly not fragile. My eyes rose to meet hers, and she must have detected a question in my gaze. "Call it a Christmas gift, call it a New Year's gift, call it whatever you want," she said, pushing it toward me with both hands.

"But I didn't get you anything. We never exchanged before," I said, feeling a bit guilty that I hadn't thought to get her anything.

"This *is* a gift for me." She settled into the back of her chair. "You'll see when you open it."

It was wrapped in pink and purple floral paper, tied with a pink organdy ribbon, all very unseasonable, all very unDorothea.

"What, did you run out of Christmas wrap?"

"Just open it."

I unwrapped it gingerly to reveal a cardboard box with a lid. Although I admired the enthusiasm of those who tore, I was never a tearer myself. There was something that seemed disrespectful about it. I looked to see if Dorothea's face would reveal anything before I took off the lid.

"Go on," she beckoned with her hand, as if I were making too much of it all.

I took the lid off and pulled back the tissue paper. It took me a second to process that it was anything beyond four or five hundred sheets of 8 ½-x-11 paper. Then my eyes focused on the letters: A Novel (Yet to be Titled) by Dorothea Fredericks. I looked up at her in amazement. "What is this?" I asked, the surprise in my voice altering the way I normally sounded.

"You can read."

"You told me you didn't write anymore. You told me you would always be honest with me. And that's what you told me."

"I am always honest with you."

"But I asked you once if you ever thought about writing."

"I know," she said, leaning forward. "I remember. And I told you, 'All the time.' And I do, Ellen. I think about it all the time. It wasn't a lie." She sat quietly for a minute, watching me.

I could feel a transition stirring inside me. I was amazed, yes, but there was something unflattering creeping into my conscience. I didn't want her or anyone else looking at me at that moment, but still she watched. This went on for an eternity before she spoke. "Come with me for a minute," she said, swiftly rising from her chair.

I followed her to a closet. She opened the door to reveal at least seven or eight other manuscripts on a shelf. "If you had asked me if I write, I would have told you that I do, all the time."

"I don't understand how it would never come up though, how you never mentioned it in passing even."

"I didn't mean to be cagey, Ellen. Writing has always been a bit of a private struggle for me. You must have known that. I was always at my best if I was left alone with it. It felt more comfortable as a hobby all these years than a career." She turned her eyes from the manuscripts and looked at me. "I thought you'd be happy."

"I am. I'm just a little surprised, that's all. I guess I feel a little blindsided. Maybe a little alienated from an important part of your life? … I don't know." I did know I didn't want to talk about it, whatever it was, so I walked back to the manuscript on the table and started flipping through it. "What's it about?" I asked.

But she didn't answer. She had slipped into a state of pensiveness. With Dorothea, things that couldn't be seen had faces. The intangibles were always concrete enough to grasp if she thought hard enough. And right now her razor-sharp perceptiveness was slicing right through me. "Could it be that you didn't want me to *need* to write? It was more comfortable for you to see me as not *needing* anything?"

I could feel the heat rising in my cheeks, a shamefulness taking root under my skin, and I knew that she had located some of the poison, even though I was just coming to terms with its existence.

"Is that it?" she asked.

I looked up at her. "I *am* happy for you, Dorothea," I said, feeling the pools well up in my eyes. "It's not that I'm not happy for you."

"I know, baby," she cooed, walking toward me. The sudden sing-song quality to her voice surprised me. She was never one to openly express compassion, or sympathy, or deep sorrow, and it was my immediate inclination to suspect that she was mocking me. She sat next to me and placed her hand over mine, and I could feel her arm drape around the back of my chair, which left little doubt that she was sincere.

Her long fingers began massaging my hand as she continued. "I'm going to take a stab at this," she said, "but while I speak I want you to remember that what you're feeling right now, it's not wrong, it's not right ... it's just what you're feeling, Ellen. Are you with me on that?" There was a firmness about the question, and I had to nod to indicate that there was comprehension before she continued. "They say you don't truly become an adult until you see the flaws in a parent. Did you ever hear that?"

I didn't answer her. I knew if I did my voice would crack.

"I think it's true," she continued. "And you never had the chance to experience it. And now I'm going to flatter myself by suggesting that some part of you perhaps sees me as a parent figure."

"I don't know if that's true," I spoke up in defense of myself. I don't know why I was fighting it, because, God damn it, she was right of course. I probably had gotten used to looking to her for some kind of guidance. Somewhere along the way I got close to her. I had grown to rely on her as a truth-bearing constant. I don't know how I let it happen. It was embarrassing. "*You* pursued our friendship," I continued. "I wasn't looking for anything, let alone a parent. Remember?"

"Do you think I'm suggesting that you were looking for a parent? Not at all," she said, turning her head slowly from side to side. "Just listen to what I'm saying, and then you can decide what's true.

"As far as futures go, you think you lack a reference point. Most are lucky enough to see at least one person they love grow old. Most people are in a position to identify desirable aspirations by observing the lives of those who have gone before them. You lack these people in your life, and you relish seeing me as a happy, comfortable ... maybe even immensely satisfied individual. It gives you hope for your own future, doesn't it? I'm still all of those things, Ellen. If you see me that way, that makes me happy. But I want you to see me as one other thing too. I want you to see me as human. Someone who needs to mix things up once in a while. Someone who needs to challenge herself once in a while. That need never fully goes away. It tiptoes back into your life as you change. And there will always be change. It's not something to be feared. It's actually quite wonderful. It means you're ticking. And it's more than a beating heart. You're living. You can relate to all of these things. Who knows more about making change work than you?

"It's time for you to realize that you already have reference points within your life. *You've* lived. *You've* changed. *You've* challenged yourself, more than most people ever do. You have won my sincerest respect, for what that's worth to you. That's why I want to share this book with you."

I could feel my tear-streaked face break into a salty smile, conceding that there was no point in disagreeing with her.

"I am betting there's more too," she said. "There's something you're not telling me." And there was. The rest was even harder to talk about.

"So how do you know these things?" I asked with a small laugh.

"Human nature is the hobby of every fiction writer." She cocked a smile after she said it, and once again it was hard to know at that instant whether she was serious or not. She must have read the uncertainty on my face. "I don't *know* these things," she said. "I'm just taking a stab at them, that's all. And you know me, I have to speak what's on my mind. It has to come out, more often getting myself into trouble for it than not."

"I was wrong to feel betrayed by you."

"No," she said, cutting me off right away. "It's what you were feeling. We can't help what we feel."

"I want the tables to turn. I don't want to be the one always on display. You've dissected almost everything about me. What is in your past?" I asked, wiping my face with the back of my hand. "You never talk about it."

"You will see a lot of me in here," she said, releasing my hand to tap the top of the manuscript.

"So what does this mean?" I asked, picking the manuscript up, beginning to feel something with endless promise in its weight. "You want my opinion?"

"Not really." I looked at her in time to catch the smile lines rippling up her cheeks. "You know I'm too stubborn to change it. It's exactly what I want it to be. It's ... genuine." We both knew she was robbing John, which brought an easy smile to my face.

"Imitation is the highest form of flattery," she said. "I want you to read it, for one, and if you like it, you can go ahead and publish it."

"Publish it?" I asked, the words falling out of my mouth with overwhelming disbelief.

"Yes."

"If I like it?"

"Yes."

"Dorothea, you know perfectly well that your novel could suck and we'd still publish it."

"There is one stipulation. There is no *we* here. I want *you* to publish it."

"Me? You know this isn't a book I'll be managing. You know it will go to a more senior editor. Good God, it will probably go to Elliot himself!"

She leaned forward and looked me straight in the eyes. "No Ellen, no book."

"You can't be serious," I said, feeling the corners of my lips curling.

"Oh, but I am," she said, raising the infamous eyebrow.

"It's completely scandalous. You can't do this for me. Don't do this for me. You have to do this for yourself."

"Like I said, it is a gift for me too." For a few seconds we just looked at each other. I guess she was waiting for a response. I guess I was waiting for the magnitude of it all to sink in. "Are you in?" she asked.

I looked down at the manuscript in my lap while my thumbs flipped through the rough edges, an attempt to determine the depth of what I was getting into. I knew I'd have to give her an answer when I looked up. There should be no hesitation, right? It's a no-brainer, right? But there was hesitation. I had been thinking about stirring things up lately too. I looked up and began to explain the rest of what I was feeling, the *more* part, the embarrassing part, the part that kept swirling in my head like oil on a Van Gogh canvas.

□

Halfway to the farm I pulled over to call Julie. I couldn't wait another minute to share the news with her. She always worked Christmas week. No one around to bug her, she always said. But she didn't answer. Knowing I would lose cell reception at the farm, I gave her Clem's phone number.

"Just ask for El, okay? No *Ellen*. No *Bannister*. You know, just El. That's how they know me. They've never asked more than that. And I haven't worked all the sticky stuff out yet. Soon though. I will tell him soon. Maybe today. But give me a ring when you get this. There's something important I need to discuss with you." I spoke quickly, hoping she would hear the excitement in my voice. I stalled for a minute toward the end, wondering what I could say to get her to call me back quickly, but there was no way to sum it up over voice mail. So I rushed through two final sentences: "I have a proposition for you. Call me."

Chapter 16

Disclosure

Twenty minutes later I was sitting in my car at the top of Clem's drive, the birds mocking me with their squawks, students of Clem, preaching of the uselessness of modern technological advances. I fiddled with the phone for a second anyway, hoping a light would come on, before realizing that there were voices in the distance. There were people talking in the barn. There was clanking too. I got out of the car and started walking toward them. As I got closer I realized, to my amazement, that the voices belonged to Clem and Finn. They were having a conversation, a steady one too, one not marred by the unpredictable waxing and waning of discord. As I inched closer I could hear bits and pieces of what they were saying.

"This we can use. This is still good. This, although not dented, is completely rusted through, so we'll have to order another."

"I'll place an order with Jake next week," Clem responded. "What's the number on that one?"

Good God, they were working on the bike. I began to creep closer when the phone slipped out of my hand. *Shit. Was the fall loud enough? Did they hear me?*

Seconds later Finn emerged in the cavernous opening. "El," he said, placing his hands on his hips. He had a wrench in his hand, and I was intimidated by the pose, thinking no one should be able to balance a wrench on their hip with nothing more than two fingers holding it in place.

"Warm day for the end of December," I said.

"Crazy, isn't it?"

I was in the middle of trying to impress him with my knowledge of global warming when I noticed something extending from under his sleeve, something stretched tightly across his skin. "Is that a nicotine patch?" I asked, unable to muffle a breath of disbelief.

"Flu shot," he fired back in half a beat, challenging me with his eyes to disagree with him.

"Is that El?" Clem called from inside.

"It's me," I yelled, not willing to tread past Finn. "Sorry to interrupt. Just trying to get a signal on my cell."

Clem emerged from the barn, hoisting the back of his pants up by the belt loops. If he were anyone else, I may have been repulsed, but I found everything Clem did adorable.

"Those things are useless," he complained. "Go on in the house and make the call from a real phone." I smiled as a vision of his clunky yellow wall phone entered my mind, the wallpaper cut sloppily around the base of it. "I'll come join you in a minute. Spot a tea sounds good." He turned to Finn, who was sliding his patched arm into the sleeve of his jacket. "What do you say we wrap this up in a few minutes? We can finish tomorrow."

"That works. Getting cold out here anyway," Finn responded, shooting me a look.

☐

Pru was leaning against the sink, sliding a dish towel around a plate, when I walked into the kitchen. "What happened?" I asked.

Her eyes flew open. "Did you see them out there?"

"Pru," I said, in utter disbelief, "they're working on the bike."

"They've been out there for the last two hours."

"How did this happen?"

"It was the strangest thing. None of us saw it coming. We were opening Christmas gifts on Christmas Eve, like we always do, and Finn hands Clem this gift, wrapped in brown paper. I don't know where he got the paper, 'cause he's usually running around here like a chicken without a head, looking for some Christmas wrap at the last minute. When I saw the brown paper and the red ribbon, I started to get this feeling, like something wonderful was about to happen. I just knew he had put real thought into the gift. It was a manual, one for that specific bike," she said, pointing toward the barn, "so that they could fix it together."

"And they've been out there most of the afternoon, just trying to figure out what they need to get that old thing running again," Nanny chimed in. I flew around at the sound of her voice. I hadn't noticed her sitting in the corner when I walked in.

"They're trying to keep as many of the original parts as they can," Pru added.

"I'm stunned," I said.

"You could have knocked me over with a feather," Nanny said.

That wouldn't be too hard, I thought.

"You should've seen Clem's face when he opened it," Pru continued. "Finn said nothing more than, 'We'll do it together,' and then he left."

"Clem's eyes were so moist I thought he'd put out the fire," said Nanny.

"It was a beautiful thing," said Pru. The three of us jumped at the snap of the screen door, and the stir of nonchalant activity began. It was as if we were all deathly afraid of upsetting a delicate balance. In sauntered Clem, as happy as a clam.

"El, would you do me the great honor of joining me for tea?" he asked, turning on the kettle.

"I just boiled that, Clem," Pru said. "It's ready."

"Today feels special," he said, rubbing his hands together. "Let's have tea in the sitting room. Pru, I'm clean enough, don't you think?" he asked, turning in a full circle for Pru's inspection.

"That's fine, Clem," she said, shaking her head, not really looking at him at all. For once, it didn't matter. As far as she was concerned, he could sit wherever he wanted. She would do nothing to dampen his spirits. It was as if Clem's time had come, and no one could argue it. Clem started to prepare a tray, but Pru waved him off, saying she'd bring it out to us.

The sitting room was a pretty room, too pretty to go unused for long. But it *had* gone unused, I was guessing for years. I was guessing that they stopped using it for entertainment purposes a long time ago. As we entered the room, I took in as much of it from a standing position as I could. Much of the left wall was home to Clem's collection of books. It was the only sign that someone may have reason to visit the room once in a while. I scanned the spines quickly, finding what appeared to be an even distribution of novels, biographies, and memoirs, all encased in beautiful white cabinetry that kept the room bright in spite of the overcast afternoon. The large windows on the right, the front side of the house, offered the existing daylight a more generous welcome than the two windows at the rear of the room, which were canopied by a large tree at the side of the house. The walls were cornflower blue, encouraging a serenity that invited reflection.

I sat on the plush blue-and-cream striped sofa with all the anticipation of a young girl invited to her first afternoon tea. I waited for Clem to sit next to me. I wanted to hear everything from his viewpoint now. No more second-hand stories. But he stood there, looking out the window. *Let him savor it, El. Don't rush him.* But I was bursting inside. How did he perceive Finn's gesture? Would it have longstanding effect? Or did he perceive it to be impulsive? Something fragile? I began pondering the answers. I so wanted to know what he thought. Everything about his demeanor suggested that he considered this action to be a turning point.

"El, you're not going to believe it," he said, turning to me. Pru came in with a serving tray, and I think he could have regained his focus easily enough had Pru been the only distraction, but then the phone started ringing. He looked to the end table, where a blue rotary phone sat. I read his face. He was being pulled in two entirely different directions, but he was happy, so happy. "I'll get it, Pru," he said.

Nanny came in with a plate of cookies, even though Pru had already plated more than enough for us in the line of sweets. There was a raspberry sponge cake sprinkled with shredded coconut and several slices of Pru's orange poundcake. "Oh, Nanny, I don't think we'll need all those," Pru said, clearly surprised by the arrival of the additional plate.

There was suddenly a lot going on, and as entertaining as the exchange between Nanny and Pru was, the phone call began taking precedence.

"Who's calling please?" Something about the cracking of Clem's voice made me nervous, but when I looked at him I was instantly calmed. He seemed relaxed, as if he were basking in a warm memory. I watched his face fill with merriment, the color rising in his cheeks. I could feel the curl on my lips. His pleasure had a way of dancing around my heart, and I watched him with great interest. But nothing could prepare me for what came next.

"Ellen Bannister?" he asked softly, his face questioning whether he had heard the voice on the other end correctly. I could feel the temperature in my blood drop, and as I rose it felt as though the blood had drained right out of me. I started walking toward him, but I have no recollection of what my intention was. Everything was overshadowed by what came next. "I don't know quite how to tell you this," he said, "but Ellen Bannister died more than twenty years ago." At that, the darkness came and my legs fell from under me.

□

"Maybe she has her period," I heard Nanny say. "That used to happen to me. All of a sudden the blood would drain from my head and I'd be down on the floor. I bet that's it. Look, she's coming to!"

I opened my eyes to see Nanny's wrinkled face hovering above me, her eyes squinting through her smudged wire-rimmed glasses, straining not to miss anything. Pru was there too, stretching around Nanny, her face etched with concern. Someone else was coming into focus too, just to the right of Pru. The frame was too broad to be Clem. *Don't be Finn. Don't be Finn. Please don't be Finn.* But it was, of course. I looked down to see his hands supporting a pillow at my feet. I thought if I looked at him long enough I would realize what was happening. His would be the face with answers. He looked apprehensive at first, stuck in a position of waiting. Not one of great patience, and certainly not one to find pleasure in speculation, he was of the nature that would always find a position of waiting difficult. For this reason alone, it is thoroughly bizarre that I would find any comfort in the carved lines of anxiety and frustration I found on his face, but I know that I did.

"Stand back, Nanny! Give her some air," he scolded.

And as she did, a fourth individual came into view. It was Clem. *Oh good, Clem is here too,* I remember thinking. But he didn't look himself. Something didn't feel quite right. There was something that I had never seen in his face, a face that had grown so familiar to me. There was concern, but there was something else there too. *A tinge of embarrassment? Was that it?*

"Are you all right, Ellen?" he asked. The other three heads turned to look at him. *Had they detected something a bit off too?*

I suddenly felt an intense need to sit up, to figure out why I was lying there to begin with. I rose quickly but was gently halted by Finn, his hand on my forearm. "Easy, El. Not too fast now."

Then Nanny, wanting to contribute, said, "Yeah, that's right. Easy now, El ..." She paused as if she wasn't quite finished, and I saw her head take on a quizzical tilt as she turned toward Clem and muttered, "len?" That's all it took, and then it all came flooding back to me.

I looked at Clem, whose eyes were locked on me. I suppose he saw the recognition on my face. He inched closer. "Are you all right?"

"Yes," I said faintly, feeling like my voice wasn't my own anymore. I never thought it would happen this way. I just thought one day, in my own time, I would tell him that he writes to me. I just thought I would go on telling little white lies until I was ready. All to stay close to him. And now I wasn't even sure he was writing to me. There was only one thing I could think to say. "Did somebody die?" I asked. Finn, Pru, and Nanny looked to him in unison.

"Don't worry, you are alive and well, as you probably already figured out," he said, waving his hand as he said it, as if this were just a minor detail. "And thank God you are," he said. He still looked a little uneasy, but at least there was a small smile as he turned away. "Come up and see me once you've had a chance to rest a little," he called over his shoulder.

□

I climbed the stairs slowly. My legs felt like lead. As hard as it was for my body to move, I couldn't slow the filmstrip that was flying through the reel in my head. Some people say that you see your life flash before you when you're approaching death. Clem had assured me that I was alive and well. So why couldn't I stop the filmstrip?

The images came quickly. I saw my mother, smiling at me sweetly as she waved goodbye with one hand and held tight to Johnnie with the other. I didn't want them to leave. They had dropped me off at the sleepover, and they were waving goodbye as they walked down the hall together. I was puzzled, because that never actually happened. I didn't even say goodbye to my mother that day. But here I was saying goodbye. I was in the frame of the apartment door, watching her walk away. "Don't worry, Ellen," she was saying. "You'll have fun, darling. We'll see you tomorrow."

I could see my father too, in later footage, stooping outside the passenger window when I pulled the car up to the curb, asking the instructor if I had passed the road test. It didn't make sense. Johnnie had done that. But now Johnnie was in the backseat, congratulating me that I had indeed passed. And then suddenly it wasn't the driving instructor that was seated next to me. It was Finn. He had come along for the ride. I turned back to Johnnie, but he was gone. I looked out the window, but my father was gone too.

Then I could hear the train coming. It would suck me up if it could. I knew it would if it could. I turned to Finn. He was still sitting there, not realizing the danger. *What could I do?* I started yelling at him and crying: "Finn, what are you doing? It's coming. Don't you hear it?" But he just sat there, smiling, oblivious to the danger, looking the happiest I'd ever seen him. "What's the matter with you? Don't you hear it?" My mind was racing. *What could I do?* I closed my eyes and sucked in air. I sucked in air as hard as I could. I sucked him right into me, just as the train was coming. I sucked in so hard I woke myself.

I was sitting up, but I didn't know where I was. "It was just a dream, El. Do you hear me?" I turned to see Pru, sitting in an armchair next to me, her hands embracing a cup of tea. I looked around the room, letting everything that had happened sink in once again. "El, are you okay?"

"How long have I been sleeping?"

"No more than ten minutes. After Clem went upstairs, I made Finn and Nanny leave. You said you were going to rest your eyes a few minutes. Nanny and I made quite a scene when you passed out, and, well, frankly, I'm doing my best not to make one now. El ... Ellen ... are you all right? Should I call a doctor?"

"No, please don't." I sat up and placed my feet on the floor, doing my best to pull it together quickly. The last thing I wanted at this point was a doctor. "It's more of a procrastination problem than anything else."

"A procrastination problem?" She looked at me as if I had two heads.

"I just need to talk to Clem. I'll be fine after that." I turned to face her. "Pru, there's nothing wrong with me ... at least not physically." I had hoped she would crack a smile when I put my mental state into question, but apparently my mental state was exactly what she was worried about. "I'll be fine. Sorry to worry you. I just need to talk to Clem. I'll be fine after that." Though I wasn't quite sure that that was true. I wasn't at all sure how I would be after I talked to Clem.

"I'm sure he's still waiting for you upstairs," she said. "Go put it all to rest, whatever it is."

I started for the stairs, but I paused half way. "Sorry to have worried you."

"That's all right. Don't worry about me." She did her best to convince me that she was all right, but I could tell she didn't have much patience for this anymore. Pru was a practical woman. Kindhearted through and through, but very practical. In her mind, anything that could be resolved, should be resolved, and swiftly. She looked at me expectantly, and I had no choice but to go upstairs.

When I reached the top of the stairs, it occurred to me that I didn't know exactly where I was going. I always stayed in the first room on the left, and I had never been any farther down the hall than that. "Clem?" I called.

"Down here," he answered.

I stepped lightly down the hall, the floorboards creaking under me. The voice came from one of the rooms at the end, and when I got there I could see that he was seated at a desk in the corner, his face buried in his hands. The room was simple: buttercup wallpaper, a twin bed with a white chenille bedspread, a couple of chairs of simple wood frame, and the desk, of course. Clem was not a large man at this point in his life, and I would guess that he had never been that big in stature, but the furniture seemed dwarfed by his presence.

"Ohhh Ellen," he sighed, caressing his forehead with the tips of his fingers, the last bit of daylight from the window behind him washing over his rounded shoulders. It was not lost on me that he had addressed me by my birth name. He raised his head, his eyes staring into the buttercup wallpaper, as if it were so much more than buttercup wallpaper weathered by time. It was as if he were staring into an open field. "Here you are sitting under my nose for the past three months." He slowly turned his head from left to right and back again, as if he were seeing something he simply couldn't believe in the pattern. "God damn! No wonder I took to you so fast." He turned his head toward me, and only then did I realize the magnitude of the moment in his eyes, the leveling of our playing field. "What must you think of me?" he asked.

"I could ask the same," I tried to say, only my voice wasn't quite there. I said it again, fighting for clarity. Still didn't sound like myself though. I cleared my throat in an effort to find a voice that sounded like my own. "Couldn't I?" I asked, inching my way into the room, spurred by a sense of relief that he didn't appear angry. "I'm not exactly proud that I hid who I am from you." I sat on the edge of the bed, which was behind where he was sitting, and I waited for him to turn and face me.

He leaned back in the chair, supporting the weight of his forearms on the tips of his fingers, which tottered on the edge of the desk while all other action was suspended by his pensiveness. "You never answered my letters."

"I never had an address. You mustn't have wanted me to."

"Yet you found me."

"I only read the first two. I have five unopened letters in my bag."

"Why?" he asked incredulously, finally turning to me.

"I ask myself that very question all the time. I even talk to my friend Dorothea about it. It didn't feel right once I knew you, for one. That's what I told myself for a long time. I was really proud of myself too. I thought, *How noble of me.*" I could feel an uncomfortable laughter welling up, and I knew I was heading off on a tangent. *Focus, Ellen, focus. He deserves it.* Then there was so much focus that I started rapidly spurting the truth. "Then I realized it was probably more about fear than anything else. My friend Dorothea knew this from the get-go. I really liked you. I looked forward to seeing you. I didn't want to learn anything negative before I had to. It's like I'm living a fantasy life here, Clem. You're wonderful to me. It's great. I didn't want it to end. Does that make sense?"

"What makes you think there's something negative to come?"

"Because it couldn't get better than this." His expression revealed nothing, but I could tell the notion disturbed him.

"You're about to come clean with me, and I'm not going to like what you're going to say. Right? It doesn't get better than this?"

He looked at me blankly, like he wasn't quite sure what I was getting at. "Only you can answer that."

Then he leaned over to open the bottom right drawer and pulled from it the sole contents, a manila file folder. He turned a small desk light on, pulled a chair up, and beckoned me to join him. His knobby pointer fingers tapped lightly on the folder while I settled myself next to him. "I don't want you to be afraid by anything you see here."

He opened the folder to reveal a small gathering of newspaper clippings. I could see his hands shaking now, and the mere fact that he had asked me not to be afraid made me more so. The top clipping was an obituary. I could see this much when I stretched my head over his arm. I didn't care very much about respecting his personal space just then. I kept stretching until I could see the words. It was his daughter's. I knew her first and last name. It was what came between that made me catch my breath. As if he sensed it, he turned quickly and took my hand. "Please don't be afraid. Please, Ellen. Don't be afraid. It's going to be okay."

"Judith *Bannister* Vance? We're related?"

"No," he said, shaking his head adamantly. "We're not related. Look at the date she died. You want to tell me what it means to you?"

I took a closer look at the obituary, and a sense of panic engulfed me when I realized that she died the same day that John did. I remember cupping my mouth with one hand while Clem squeezed the other. "You knew John, didn't you?"

"I didn't. I didn't know you either. My heart broke for you though." He turned his face away from me. "I just felt for you, that's all. I saw your name, and I felt for you."

"What do you mean you *saw* my name? What do you mean you just felt for me? If we're not related, then why did you feel for me? It's not like you didn't have your own loss going on."

"It's probably best if I start with the other Ellen Bannister."

"The one that died more than twenty years ago?"

"That's right," he said, smiling. "You know, I tell you about her all the time," he said, scratching the top of his ear. "You already know a lot about her. Bannister was my wife's maiden name. I married Ellen Bannister almost forty years ago, and as corny as it may sound, I'll remain married to her for the rest of my life. My relationship with you starts with her."

Whenever Clem spoke about his wife, I was riveted, but for the first time ever I grew impatient, even irritated. I wanted to say to him, *Okay, I get it. Your wife and I share the same name*—a fact that would have intrigued me at any other given moment. But at this moment, all I wanted to know was what this had to do with John. I started to ask, but he stopped me. He grabbed my forearm and said, "My relationship with you starts with her. It has nothing to do with your brother on a personal level. Nothing." I waited eagerly for more. "Nothing," he said again, as if reiteration would help pound it into me. "Nothing except that the day my baby died was the same day your brother died."

He picked up the next clipping under Judith's obituary, this one of full-page length. The bottom half of the page was a traditional obituary section, the lives of those who passed summed up in neat little boxes of varying length. Clem had circled the box dedicated to the life of his daughter, Judith Bannister Vance, but he had also circled a name on the top half of the page, the portion of the page traditionally reserved for those who may not be front-page news but those who had made a name for themselves in their respected fields nonetheless, whether that be chemistry, literature, politics, etc. I wasn't of an age where the obituary page was a common reference, but even I was familiar enough with it to have a rough idea of the format. A couple of these more prominent obituaries included photos of the featured deceased. I didn't spend much time looking at them. I was drawn to a third photograph, one that lacked the reverence of the others. I was drawn to it simply because Clem had circled the name *Ellen Bannister* in the caption.

I scanned the picture quickly, looking for a middle-aged woman, looking for a picture of his wife, even though this made little or no sense looking back on it. How could his wife, who died twenty some odd years earlier, be pictured on the same page as her daughter's obituary? It was a street scene, a sea of people in black. I jumped to the conclusion that it was a picture taken at his wife's funeral. A picture they were running again because of his daughter's death maybe? I couldn't pull all the pieces together quickly enough. Finally I read the caption: "Ellen Bannister, the sister and lone survivor of subway victim John Bannister, is comforted by a fellow mourner outside St. Ignatius Loyola Church following Monday morning's funeral service."

I had never seen the picture before, and I closed in on it, devouring every detail. There were mourners mulling about in front of the church, most of them people I didn't recognize, and there in the center I found all that was visible of me, my arms pressing into Tony's suited back. It couldn't possibly be true. I never knew a newspaper photographer had been there. "Oh my God," I muttered. "How did you get this?" I asked accusingly, rising out of my chair. It was an idiotic question. I realize that now. It's not like Clem had stolen something that belonged to me, but it felt like he had.

"It was just there, in the paper the very day I brought it back here from town, the very day I locked myself in this room to look at Judith's obituary by myself. And there you were, sort of. I don't believe in signs, Ellen, but I kept thinking my wife was trying to communicate something."

I rose out of my chair and started heading for the door, but I didn't get far before I heard Clem's chair scratch against the floor planks. "Where are you going?"

I stopped short. "I don't know where I'm going." I turned around to face him. "I have no idea where I'm going." I looked around the room just then, taking in all that I could, but there wasn't much there. I was struck by the starkness. I looked down at the planks that formed the floor, wondering where I was going and what I was running from. "There's a part of me that wants to hear you out."

"It's not like I see you as some reincarnation of my wife, or of my daughter for that matter. I'm not a crackpot." It was the way he said *crackpot* that broke my heart. It was guttural and sickening, like he was vomiting up poison. "I'm not ... should that notion be crossing your mind ... at least not in the traditional sense of the word." And I realized he was on to something. That's exactly why I wanted to leave. I was ready to sell all the good stuff down the river ... everything he had done for me, the roof he was so willing to put over my head, the help he was so willing to give me on a book that would never be written. He had hit the nail on the head. I was suddenly afraid that he was crazy. And I was ashamed that I felt this way. "You have to be patient with me. I'll tell you everything," he said.

There was no point in leaving. I wouldn't gain anything in leaving. So I walked back to the empty chair he was offering. When I sat back down he began speaking softly again. There wasn't any hesitation anymore. He was going to tell it like it was.

"When my daughter died, my first inclination was to pick up her schedule, to do the things she'd do. Somebody had to continue the things she had been doing. Obviously I couldn't go to work for her. That's not what I'm talking about." At this he flailed his hands in the air and his voice got deep and raspy, as if he were frustrated with himself, frustrated that there were limitations to what he could and could not do on her behalf. But he settled down nicely, taking on the voice of a storyteller once again. "She'd go into town when she was here, pick up a coffee, get the New York papers. I did these things for her in the days after she died. I started doing them before she was buried, for God's sake. I couldn't wait." He paused for a second and then shot me a painful look out of the corner of his eye. "There's a lot of time that takes place between a death and a funeral. Some people can't sit still and wait for a formal ritual to take place. So I picked up her routine. I needed to get out of the house. I needed to live for her, breathe for her. *You* know what I mean."

I was stunned that he brought me into the story. We weren't exactly having a conversation at this point. I expected that he'd keep talking. I didn't want to acknowledge that I actually *did* know what he meant. To my relief, he picked up his story quickly again, not waiting for me to respond.

"I needed to talk to her. I needed to feel her around me, and I thought if I did the things she did, developed her routine, I would feel her presence. And I did."

He paused briefly and then began talking in what seemed like general terms. "We all need to know someone is listening to us. I think about this all the time. It makes us feel less alone.

"I didn't have anyone to listen to me. What I did was incredibly self-serving, I mean writing to you like that. I *needed* someone to listen to me. Look around me," he said, waving his hand in the air. "I have wonderful people in my life, but the topic of death isn't easy for them. You may ask, 'Well who the hell is it easy for?' For no one. I understand that. But when you look at my group, you've got to admit that it's harder for them than most. They don't bring much comfort to a talker. It's like my thoughts on death are too painful for them to bear. And anyone outside of them never sticks around long enough for the core to come out. I don't want their pity. So even though I didn't know you, you somehow gave me something I didn't have. You listened to me, or I imagined that you did. Well, you did. At least for a little while.

"But it wasn't just selfishness on my part. I have a feeling about life that if something keeps nagging at you you have to take care of it. This is the part that isn't concrete. Sometimes we don't understand why we keep going back to something. When I first saw your name in that caption, I didn't know that I would keep thinking of you. I didn't know that I would come to a point where I would consider that our lives were parallel. My eyes just fell upon your name. I was laughing and crying at the same time. I remember pointing up at the ceiling and saying, 'What are you up to, Ellen?' In a coincidental kind of way. 'You're trying to make your presence known, aren't ya? No comments from the peanut gallery,' I told her. 'Just take care of her, okay? Wish you were here to help me, but I'd never wish this on you.' I talked to her. I always talk to her. To me, seeing your name that first day was just a little nudge from her, nothing more than that.

"But I kept the clipping anyway," he said, holding it gingerly in his hand. "We had a funeral for Judith after that. I continued driving into town every morning, getting the papers and coffee.

That went on for a few weeks. I gradually started doing my thing around here again. I didn't really talk to people beyond the everyday stuff. Getting on the phone and asking crews to come in and do a few days' work. Returning calls from vendors. That kind of thing. Nothing too difficult.

"Then I'd come in here at night," he said, turning to take in the room. "This was her room, you know," he said, shooting me a glance.

"I thought it might be," I said, softly.

"Pru got rid of her things. Never asked me if she could." He got quiet for a second, and I could see that this hurt him deeply. "She meant well, of course," he tacked on, his voice like gravel. I got on with things, but I'd come in here at night. Shut the door behind me. Flip through my clippings. This was my way of mourning. In the depth of mourning, strange things can happen. Something started tugging at me. It was gradual. I didn't look at your name and see anything beyond a coincidence in the beginning. But one night I took up this clipping and said to my wife, 'Well who is this girl?'" Then he shot me a look. "I didn't write to you right away, you know." He said this as if he knew it were in his favor, that maybe if I knew this I wouldn't think he was crazy. And I knew he spoke the truth. Several years had gone by before he wrote to me.

"A long time went by before I could see that you had a story too. Then I started focusing more on your story. The caption kept running through my mind, even when I wasn't sitting in here. I could be out in the orchard or in the truck, and I'd see those words in my head, *lone survivor*. Like you were some kind of freak. I'd say to Ellen in my head, 'Well that was unnecessary. Even if it's true, they didn't need to draw attention to it, like she's some circus act. Whatever sells papers, I suppose.' It was the first time I could feel some spunk in me again. I started to feel my blood boiling again, and the heat felt good. I could hear Ellen in my head, 'Go do something about it. You would for Judith. You're still good for somethin', old man.'

"So I did some research and started reading up on what happened to your brother." He turned to the next clipping. It was John's obituary. Strange how something that was written for all to see four years earlier felt oddly personal in his hands. He looked up at me. "Look, I have lots of clippings here, but we both know what happened." He lay his hand gently on John's obituary, compressing any of his research that lay underneath. "We don't need to sift through each piece. We know what happened to your brother. The details don't matter. The outcome's still the same. Life is about how you live, not how you die."

Then he turned to me. "Ellen had a lot of spunk. I was only 57 when she died, but she still called me 'old man.' I could hear her responding to my thoughts too, giving me a sense of empowerment again. 'You might want to write to her,' she'd say, 'tell her that she's not alone, tell her you know what she's going through. You could write to her. You might want to do that.'"

And just then I could feel something pierce me. Some familiar, uncontrollable pain started washing over me. Words started flying through my head like a torrent: *You might want to take a ride someday.* John had said this to me only a couple of times, but the message was loud and clear. It was one I kept hearing after he was gone. He was trying to empower me. People who love you like the dickens will do that. They want you to be okay forever. I could feel the significance of their words welling up inside of me, the weight of their kindness. And these lovely people, those beating hearts ... the other Ellen ... John ... they had just been looking out for us in life, unaware that their messages were like little care packages that would slip into a black hole and find us again in another place and time. Their parcels would take care of us until we could manage again. It was all about resilience, oh lovely ones!

Next thing I knew I was heaving, big heavy sobs. Clem was in the middle of saying something, but as soon as he realized he grabbed me. He leaned over and he grabbed me. He embraced me from the side and held me against him and wouldn't let go. "It's okay. It's okay, darlin', you just let it out." Our postures couldn't be more awkward too, but I didn't care. I wasn't even embarrassed by it. He held my head against his chest with one hand and wrapped his arm around my shoulders and squeezed. And he wouldn't stop. I didn't want him too either. The mustiness of his shirt almost choked me, and I didn't care. I could feel his chest hairs matted down by the weight of my forehead, and I didn't care. I wrapped my arms around him and wouldn't let go. I soaked him with my tears. If I had any sense at all I would have taken his age into consideration and recognized the threat of pneumonia. But it was a glorious moment where I think we both recognized the risks of being human, and we embraced the hell out of those risks.

Chapter 17

A New Acquaintance

I was tired after my talk with Clem, and the last thing I wanted to do was go on a blind date. I put on my own clothes this time around. That is to say that I did not wear anything I bought while shopping with Julie. I was too drained to fuss. I wore black pants, a black turtleneck top, and black loafers with a heel, pretty much the things I would wear to work. I put my hair up in a ponytail and slipped on small gold loop earrings. I applied a little blush and a little mascara, just enough to draw some attention away from the bloodshot eyes and the puffiness, the natural features I didn't care to accentuate.

As I made my way down the stairs, I could see that there was light in the sitting room. I was hoping to find Clem or Pru. I wanted to tell someone where I was going. Finn rarely occupied the house in the evenings—or in the daytime, for that matter— so I was startled to find him sitting in an armchair across from Clem. They had just started a fire and the dim light illuminated their profiles with a warm hue. Finn turned his head toward me, the light falling from one side of his face to the other.

I caught my breath and walked in. I had to. He knew I saw him. But I walked with great trepidation, mostly because I didn't have enough time to figure out what to say, but partly because I could feel my heels getting caught up in the rug.

Clem eventually caught sight of me coming. "What are your plans, my darlin'?"

"I'm going to head over to that new place, Speed's," I said, motioning direction with my hand, even though I had no clue if I was indicating the correct direction from where I was standing. There was an uneasy silence for a second. I think they were waiting to hear more, but I was reluctant to say more with Finn sitting there. I was surprised at how much I didn't want him to know I was going on a date. "Someone told me the food's pretty good there."

We continued to look at each other. "That's all," I added.

"Well have fun, darlin'," Clem finally said, his eyes soft and weary, his voice sincere. "Good to try new things."

I liked him calling me darlin'. In some way, it put the awkwardness of El and Ellen behind us. I knew eventually he would have to choose El or Ellen. He couldn't go around referring to me as darlin' forever. One would have to win out over the other, and I looked forward to knowing which one it would be.

As I turned to leave, I remembered the phone call. "Clem," I asked, "did Julie leave a message for me?"

Clem sucked in his bottom lip before he responded, as if the answer were a grain of salt he could lick up with his tongue. "Julie?"

"Yeh, the caller earlier." I could feel my face flushing. I hated bringing the whole mess up again. "The call that started the whole thing," I added.

"Oh no, that was some fellow named Elliot. Said he was your boss. Said he'd call back."

It was so typical. It all made sense to me now. Julie was too smart to slip up. I could see Elliot rummaging through Julie's things, coming across Clem's phone number with my name above it on a post-it in Julie's drawer. It was so Elliot not to think twice about invading someone's privacy. What would normally burn me up was suddenly so amusing. I wondered if Clem could detect the curl of my mouth in the dim lighting.

"Well, goodnight," I said, to both of them really, but I know my parting glance went to Finn. It's not like I gave it any thought. It just happened that way. I was a little embarrassed about it though.

"Goodnight, El," Finn called as I left the room. At least he had made up his mind. He was sticking with *El*.

□

Dorothea's friend was named Chase Champion. He would be wearing khakis, a navy blazer, and of all indiscreet things, a red tie, and he would be seated at the bar. I hated this. It was my first blind date, and I was early. I sat outside in the car for twenty minutes before making my way in, still five minutes early. But he was already there. If he was as full of anxiety as I was, I couldn't detect it. He was immediately pleasant, more so than I expected. Maybe a little more vulnerable than I expected too. His hair had begun to gray at the temples, and his smile was so warm you felt like you were receiving a piece of apple pie à la mode. He was handsome, at least by my account.

"El," he said, rising off the bar stool, sighing with relief. God knows what he was expecting, but his reception was immensely flattering.

"How did you know?"

"You're just as Dorothea described."

"Am I?" I asked, thinking Dorothea must have played me up a little, 'cause I certainly don't put much effort into my appearance for Dorothea anymore.

"Yes," he said, his eyes flying open. "She actually told me a lot about you." He slid a stool out for me as the bartender approached. "Drink?"

"But she didn't tell you what I drink, did she?" I teased.

"No, she didn't. I guess she only knows so much," he said, laughing heartily.

I ordered a chardonnay and turned my attention back to him. "I don't believe I've ever had a drink with Dorothea."

"So this could be fun then? You'll have a few more after this one and I'll fill her in on all the things she doesn't know."

"Ah, ha, ha," I said, pointing a finger at him. The conversation was surprisingly playful. "No blind-date jitters for you, are there?"

"I don't know about that," he laughed, smoothing an eyebrow with his finger. "I actually had some serious reservations, only because Dorothea speaks so highly of you and I want her to continue thinking highly of me. So you see, I'm under a lot of pressure here."

"At the risk of sounding unforgivably vain, what has she told you about me?"

"Specifics or generalizations?"

"Start with the generalizations, and we'll work our way up to specifics."

"I'll tell you what she *didn't* tell me," he laughed. "She *didn't* tell me that you enjoyed talking this much about yourself. That's for sure."

"You're right. Let's talk about you."

"Oh no you don't! Why do I feel like you just pulled a fast one on me? Let's see," he said tapping his finger on the bar. "What's safe to tell you?"

"Tell it all or say nothing at all," I laughed.

And this was how my blind date began. It was light-hearted. It was silly. In some ways, it was downright intoxicating. It was a pleasant surprise. It turned serious at moments too, which, even though he was virtually a stranger, was okay with me. I will always have a need for depth. I will always have a need to examine one layer after another. Whether the circumstances of my life dictate it or it is genetically part of my makeup, a need to be serious pulls at me intermittently whenever I get comfortable, and he seemed to know this about me.

"I'm sorry about your brother," he said. Dorothea *had* told him about me. "I have siblings, a sister and a brother, and I don't know what I'd do without them. They're like my best friends."

"I'm happy for you." The words came out sounding hollow. "It's nice when that happens." I was surprised that I didn't feel like getting into it with him just then. Maybe, for once, I had used up all my emotional reserves for one day. "You know, let's not talk about that. Let's just have fun."

"Then fun it is!" he declared, slapping his hand firmly on the bar. Then he looked at me sheepishly. "So if we were to be having fun, what would we be talking about right now?"

"My love of movies and books, your love of ..."

"Sailing and parachuting," he said, not missing a beat.

By the end of our cocktail hour, he had convinced me that he was not only well-read but well-versed on a number of topics, and we happily began our departure from Speed's for Chez O'Shea, the adventurous side in him having persuaded me that it was time to throw caution to the wind and try escargot for the first time.

Chase stopped at the coat check to retrieve his raincoat while I pressed into the door, eager to breath the invigorating late December air, but the door had already begun to open, requiring little help from me. "Where are you going?" a voice asked.

I looked to the body standing in front of me, and I know my eyes must have flown open. "Finn!" I had never seen him in a suit before, and he looked great. "What are you doing?"

"Heard the food was good here," he said, the corners of his lips forming a soft smile.

"But who are you meeting?" The words had tumbled out, and I deeply regretted asking. If I could have mauled my tongue at that instant and still be considered sane, I would have. *Just shut up, Ellen. Why do you need to know?*

He didn't concentrate too hard on answering. I saw him open the door as far as it would extend, but still I waited. Then he gently took my arm to pull me forward, his smile now dancing between puzzlement and amusement. "El, there's a gentleman behind you trying to get out."

"Oh geez, I'm sorry." I took several strides forward and turned around, only to realize that the gentleman he was referring to was Chase, who just stood there waiting, I guess for me to introduce him. "Oh my God, this is Chase!"

Finn looked at me out of the corner of his eyes before raising his hand to greet Chase, who already had his hand extended to

Finn. "Finn Vance," Finn said, coolly. Then he turned to me. "El, can I talk to you for a second?"

I'm not sure why I felt the need to refer to Chase, but I looked his way. "Please," Chase said, gesturing with his arm for the two of us to take a walk.

"I'll just be a minute," I said, but Chase had already begun walking away from us in an effort to create a polite distance.

I walked with Finn across the graveled lot until he stopped at a parked car under a weeping willow. When I looked back toward Chase I could see that the hanging tree limbs offered all the privacy of a pulled curtain.

"Are you crazy?" Finn asked, his upper body leaning toward me while his fist, bearing the weight of his irritation, pressed into the hood of a stranger's car.

"What do you mean?" I asked, almost in a whisper, hoping Chase couldn't hear us.

"Have you no sense at all? You can't just leave with some guy you just met in a bar."

"I know that." There was silence for a second.

"Care to elaborate?"

"It was a setup. He knows a friend of mine. He's perfectly safe."

As the edges of his face began to soften, his cheeks grew increasingly flushed. It was suddenly as if I were looking into the face of a young boy whose feelings had just been hurt. That's when it began to sink in. *He had come to meet me.* My heart exploded, because I would have given everything that I had to walk into Mark Speed's place, plop my bum on a barstool, and talk to Finn Vance all night. *Just say it, Finn. If it's true, can you please just say it?*

His body relaxed into his normal stance as he took the weight off his fist. I watched him glance down at his hand as he spread his fingers out like a fan. When he looked up again he had gained some composure. "Just be careful, okay?" I watched him walk away, his path curving like an arc as he made his way toward the front door of Speed's.

I made my way back to Chase, who was leaned against a car across the street. "Let me guess. The farmer's son?" he asked.

"Dorothea told you about him too?

"Sort of. She grossly underestimated his pull on you."

"Is it that obvious?"

"I'm not an idiot. You'd have to be one to miss it."

"I just feel so stupid. It's such a roller-coaster ride. I think he came here to see me tonight, but am I sure? No. God forbid he say it!" Then I realized how ridiculous it was to be confessing this to my date. "Sorry," I said, lamely.

"If he can't commit to you, then why should you commit to him? Come have dinner and we'll talk about it." When I didn't respond immediately, he tacked on, exasperatedly, "It's just a dinner!"

So we did have dinner, but the escargot wasn't what I thought it would be. The evening had already been soured. It was probably really good escargot too, but it had been wasted on me.

After dinner he drove me back to Speed's and walked me to my car. "Look, Ellen, this is clearly something you need to explore, so go ahead and do it. We just met. I'm a big boy. If it doesn't work out with him, give me a call."

"Okay," I said, but I could barely look at him I was so embarrassed about all that had transpired. He began to walk away, and I called after him, "Thanks for dinner."

He turned back around and stood there, just looking at me. Then he walked back, nuzzled his cheek against mine, long enough so that I could feel the warmth of his breath on my ear, and whispered, "I would like to do more than this, but circumstances preclude my doing so." He kissed my cheek and left, for good this time.

The road home was lovely, dark, and deep, and I had absolutely no promises to keep. I flipped the high beams on, slid the Beatles greatest hits into the CD player, forwarded to "The Long and Winding Road," and wondered why we make the choices we do.

□

The light was on in the kitchen when I got back to Clem's. As I walked in I could hear someone rustling in the sitting room. I waited in the kitchen, since there was no light on in the sitting room. And momentarily Finn emerged.

"Are you divorced?" he asked. He was standing on the other side of the table now, a hand gripping one of the chair backs, the veins on the underside of his arm bulging. The rigidness of his body defied his eyes, which were soft, even pleading. I felt like I was dreaming.

I must have given him a searching look, a look that was asking him where the question was coming from, because right then he held up the folder. Clem's folder. My folder. Clem's folder on me. He had been reading about me. The answers to my everything in a manila folder, and he was clutching it so hard it was bending under the pressure. My mind started racing. What had he seen? The picture outside the church? No, I wasn't wearing a ring. I was separated then. The obituary? Maybe. I was willing to bet he had gotten his hands on John's obituary, which may have mentioned a surviving brother-in-law. I'm sure I mentioned Brian in the obituary. He deserved to be mentioned.

I was a little annoyed, and ashamed too. I hated talking about my divorce. "Yes," I answered, "I'm divorced." I know I made an attempt to explain what he had seen, to tell him about Brian, but it was as if the details didn't matter.

"The man you were just with?" he interrupted.

"Yes?"

"Who was he?"

"Blind date. Never saw him before. Probably never see him again." I wasn't proud of myself for downplaying that there was actually an attraction to Chase, but I wanted to give him every opportunity to express interest. My heartbeat was all I could hear in the stillness of the room. Then I gulped involuntarily and asked, "Why were you there?"

He never acknowledged the question. It was as if he never heard it. He began walking toward me with great purpose. The force of his rush pinned me to the wall, and his hands quickly moved from my waist to my face. The warm pulse of his fingers was there again, just as it had been before. "Don't go anywhere," I whispered. "Don't start something you can't finish."

But he didn't stop there like he did before. Instead he took my hand, pulled me outside, and guided me through the darkness, up the long and winding road that led to his door.

Chapter 18

Springtime

There was a thickness about the evening air that made me question why I had stayed so long at work. It takes me a while to get my things together on a Thursday night anymore. I only go into the office three days a week now, and if I forget something on a Thursday I won't see it again until Tuesday morning. It was amazing how flexible the hierarchy had become when presented with another Dorothea Fredericks' novel. The book had exactly the type of clout Dorothea had hoped it would. I didn't want to take advantage of it all the same, but I would be lying if I said I wasn't grateful to pursue other interests on Mondays and Fridays.

I was just reaching the street when the sky broke open. Big, thick drops at first. Then the sheets came. I watched for a minute before deciding to retreat to the elevator bank. Of all the things I managed to remember, an umbrella was not one of them.

I moved rhythmically and somewhat impatiently on the balls of my feet while I waited for the elevator, that is until I sensed another body had joined me. I didn't look to see who it was. Riding the elevator at work was somewhat comparable to riding a New York City subway. For better or worse, you normally lack interest in making eye contact with your fellow passengers. Unlike the subway, however, here you do a quick peripheral scan, and then your brain decides within a fraction of a second whether the frame of the individual warrants a slight head motion for further identification.

I pressed 30 and claimed my corner of the elevator before turning my focus to the floor panel, because the floor panel, by the way, is a perfectly comfortable visual point of reference. It offers some small piece of information about your fellow passenger, in a vague sort of way, while one's focus on the floor panel conveys a subtle disinterest in fellow passengers, which seems to go over well among New Yorkers in close quarters. When no other floor lit up, I could see that my fellow passenger was headed for the same destination, Burke and Patterson, and I wondered who he was.

My speculation only intensified when he defied all unspoken rules by blatantly staring at me.

"You're the mystery sibling."

I searched his face, my eyes absorbing every detail, before reaching the conclusion that he had to have said something else and that I was crazy, someone who imagines the words she wants to hear. It was a slow-motion moment. I had watched his mouth move. He had said *something*. But what?

"I beg your pardon?" I finally mustered.

"You're Ellen. Ellen Bannister," he said. "The mystery sibling," he added, softness filling the words like down in a pillow.

"Do we know each other?"

"I'm sorry, Ellen. Forgive me," he said, stretching out his hand to me. "It's more like I know you, I guess. John was a very good friend of mine. I'm Chris, Chris Birchovsky."

My heart shifted to the center of my chest, the core of my being, and began thumping again, softly at first but then growing stronger, more confident. While feeling all of this I could say nothing. He wasn't as I remembered him on the television screen at Triumph so long ago. He appeared sober, for one, but there were so many other changes. His face was more chiseled. In fact, his whole body was. I never would have recognized him, but it was indeed him. I could do nothing but stand there with my mouth agape, marveling at this spectacular transformation.

"I'm sorry," he said. "I startled you."

"Birchie," I said, my voice cracking.

His face grew pale and soft. "Your brother called me that."

"I know. Oh Birchie, you have no idea how I know." The doors opened and we stepped off the elevator together.

We both stood there for a minute in the reception area, just looking at each other, I suppose trying to figure out where to go next. At least I was. It's not like we were old friends. "I thought I'd never meet you," I finally said.

"We have met, Ellen, but of course you wouldn't remember. I went to the wake. I talked with you for a minute there. Of course I went to the funeral. I didn't talk to you there. It would have been wrong to take up any more of your time. Lots of people wanted to comfort you."

"Birchie, you have no idea," I said, finding a tissue to wipe my eyes. "I kept hearing John say your name in my head. You were one of the people I wanted to meet. And here you are," I said. "What are you doing here?"

At that Jules entered the reception area in latex pants and a matching warm-up jacket. She placed her duffle bag on the swivel chair that once belonged to her and began working her hair into a ponytail. She still made herself at home in the reception area, so much so that I had to remind myself several times a week that I would no longer find her there on a regular basis. Dorothea and I were able to convince Elliot that Jules was needed for a variety of administrative tasks if we were going to publish one novel after another in such rapid succession, and that these tasks would warrant the privacy of a modest office.

Her cheeks blushed and the corners of her mouth curled, in a flirty kind of way, like she was the cat that just swallowed the canary. "So you've met."

"What do you mean?" I asked.

"This is Chris," she said. "The guy I told you about."

I was dumbfounded. I had absolutely no idea who she was talking about, and it must have shown.

"You know," she said, "a few months ago."

I could feel my blood grow warm under my skin as I recalled her sobbing in that very reception chair, and suddenly the reasons for Birchie's physical transformation could not have been clearer to me.

"Jules," I said, hoping she would feel the weight of my words, "this is Birchie." She looked toward Birchie, then back at me, disbelief emanating from her eyeliner-laden eyes. "Noooooo way!"

"Yes," I said, with cautionary terseness, trying to tell her not to mess with this particular man's heart.

"You're Birchie?" she asked, meekly, her face relaxing into a soft glow. Then she ran to him before he responded. "All this and you're Birchie too?"

"Yeah," he said, almost inaudibly, as if this fact were only meant for her. She wrapped her hands around the back of his neck, and he leaned down to kiss her.

I could feel every muscle in my body begin to relax with the sudden realization that I was witnessing genuine mutual affection, perhaps even much more. I could feel a smile spread across my face as I thought of what fun I would have sharing this news with my favorite skeptic. *Tell me again, Finn Vance, tell me again that you believe in mere coincidences. And I will have to argue, once again, that there is no such thing.*

Chapter 19

Easter

Clem said he felt comfortable standing in the back of a church on Easter Sunday, and other Sundays here and there when he was inspired to go to church. "Sometimes my spirituality takes place right here at home though." While regular church-going people might laugh or scoff at such a notion, I knew he spoke it from the heart, with complete sincerity and respect. "Taking part in the mass is a ritual, and rituals are important," he continued. "They offer a sense of common ground, a declaration of camaraderie for many. Sometimes a ritual helps move us from one place to another, helps ease the transition a little." He was putting the knot in his tie as he spoke. I went to the stove to pour him a cup of tea. It was 5:30 in the morning. I had told him I couldn't sleep, which was a lie that I could live with. "But this year, darlin', my Easter Sunday service will take place on the back of a bike," he said.

I already knew this, of course. Finn had already told me what was going on. So I just smiled at him, happy this day had come for him, happy it had come for me too. The journey he was about to take was part of my own.

Finn came in bearing a couple of helmets. "You ready, Pop?"

Clem took a big gulp of the tea and looked up at me. "I'll have to finish that later, darlin'." He was still calling me darlin', and I was beginning to hope he always would. "We've got a ride to take, a tribute to another little darlin'."

I followed them out the side door. Finn had been able to convince him, quite easily too, that this was a ride they should be taking together. I don't think either one was aware that I was there, watching them from the side of the house, away from the light that poured out of the screen door. Finn threw his leg over the bike like he had done it a million times before. Probably had. I was pretty sure, too, that he had taken the bike for several test drives on his own. "I love my old man," he had told me several months earlier, begrudgingly. I trusted then what I know now, and I was humbled to bear witness to it. Clem climbed on, placing his arms around Finn like he had done it a million times before. Probably had, albeit not in a long time. Who knows how many times a loving parent holds a child before a need for independence kicks in?

Once again, I watched the taillight until it was out of sight. I took the last sip of tea and took a deep breath, inhaling all the promise dawn had to offer before I went inside. I had my own ride to take, after all.

As I took the steps two at a time, I thought about how life is a series of ups and downs, and you pretty much had to make a decision whether to engage or not, to embrace it wholeheartedly, all its valleys and peaks, or to be satisfied with waiting for the shining moments that accidentally happen. Many are more content with the latter. You can still have a decent life this way. It works for some. I can't judge it. But I had come to realize that John was right about me. I needed to embrace all of it. For me, the valleys had proven to be a place that bettered my peaks. I lost, and I survived. I'll fall again, and I'll get up again, probably a good number of times before it's over. On this day, the sun is coming up on a new era. As I headed for the room at the top of the stairs, I started speaking to John. I am still always speaking to him.

I don't spend a lot of time on subway platforms anymore, Johnnie. I think you'd be proud of that. I've come to learn that traveling through underground tunnels would never take me where I wanted to go. But you always knew that about me, didn't you, Johnnie? I'm more like a horse coming into the backstretch now, only there is no racetrack, no boundaries, and no strong fear of losing. For I have come to know that losing is absolutely inevitable. I am just very grateful to be going for a ride. So hold on tight, Johnnie. Don't go anywhere. I'm just coming into the backstretch, and I'm about to pick up speed.

Within breaths I was sitting at the computer in front of a blank screen, my fingers galloping across the keyboard at a blistering pace, the sound of relentless hooves in my head. I produced five words for a start, the beginning of many more: MUSINGS OF A MYSTERY SIBLING.

SPECIAL THANKS

I have to start right at the beginning here. I have two of the most marvelous parents you could meet. Both are optimistic, cheerful people. Neither one was ever inclined to crush dreams. My mother, in particular, used to tell me I could do whatever I set my mind to, and my father kept me laughing. In my love for keeping things simple, I don't set my mind to doing many things! The idea to write a novel was one that wouldn't go away. So I say Thank You to Mom & Dad. You mean the world to me.

I would be remiss not to thank my early readers: Lolo, Catherine, Liz, and Nancy. Aspiring novelists are fragile people, and your words of encouragement gave me the confidence to keep going.

I owe special thanks to Harry Vance of Pochuck Valley Farms in Glenwood, NJ, and thanks to his daughters, Michelle and Diane. These people have been in the business of apple farming a very long time, and I am grateful for their time and expertise.

My thanks to Peter Schaefer of Circle Cycle in Ridgefield, NJ, for talking to a girl who knows absolutely nothing about motorcycles. Maybe one day I will ride one!

Vikki Sheatsley, my very best friend in the business. Thanks for always having interest in my story.

My thanks to eagle-eyed Trish Moroney!

I am deeply grateful to have known the real-life Julie Murphy.

My gratitude to my relatives and friends, particularly my brother's friends. Thank you for your stories, your love, and your companionship in the darkest hours. It makes me so happy and proud to look at you all and say, "They are Mike's legacy."

Thanks to my husband, such a good egg.

The author with her brother Michael.

Marian Armstrong's brother Michael was killed in the attack on the World Trade Center on September 11, 2001. *Musings of a Mystery Sibling* is a fictional account that is drawn from her real-life experiences with sibling loss.

Armstrong began a career in publishing at Macmillan in 1990. She later joined Marshall Cavendish as a reference editor of encyclopedias for elementary and high school students. *Musings of a Mystery Sibling* is her first novel. An excerpt of the work received an honorable mention from *New Millennium Writings*. She lives in New York's Lower Hudson Valley with her husband and daughter.